Victoria Marmot

and the

Inconvenient Prophecy

Virginia McClain

This is a work of fiction. Names, characters, businesses, governments, events, and incidents are the products of the author's imagination. Any resemblance to actual persons, living or dead, or actual events is purely coincidental.

Cover design by Natasha Snow

Works by Virginia McClain

The Victoria Marmot series:
Victoria Marmot and the Meddling Goddess
Victoria Marmot and the Inconvenient Prophecy
Victoria Marmot and the Shadow of Death
Victoria Marmot Book 4 is coming soon!

The Chronicles of Gensokai series:
Blade's Edge
Traitor's Hope

Short Stories
*Rain on a Summer's Afternoon**
*Note that you can get Rain on a Summer's Afternoon for free by subscribing to Virginia's newsletter

To Corey, for being a true partner.

"UMM… NICE TO see you too, Algie." My tone may have been less than sincere. As you might expect from someone who found herself with a gun pointed at her chest by one of her few remaining relatives.

"I'm terribly sorry, Vic. I wouldn't be doing this under normal circumstances, but… I'm being coerced."

"Ok. That doesn't really make me feel any better about the hot lead you could pour into my chest at any moment, but I appreciate that it's bugging you."

Algernon had always been cordial with me, and he was, in fact, my great-uncle, not my uncle, though as a kid I'd never known the distinction. He was my dad's father's brother, and even though we'd never spent a ton of time together, I'd never gotten the impression that he wanted me dead before.

"Come outside, Vic, and close the door behind you. I really don't want to shoot you, but I won't have any choice. They put a godsdamned compulsion spell on me."

I nodded, wondering what the point of getting me outside was if the plan was just to shoot me anyway. If they were willing to risk my getting shot due to non-compliance, then what was the end goal? Or was Algernon just trying to get me outside and doing a bad job of coming up with lies? Knowing that no one in the kitchen could see me from where they were, I decided to share some intel with Trev as I stepped out the front door.

Kidnapping commencing in 3… 2… 1.

What?! Trev's thoughts conveyed shock and disbelief. *Vic, what the fuck!? Is Algernon taking you somewhere?*

But even as Trev's reply entered my mind, Algernon was reaching back with the hand holding the gun, tears streaming down his face as he brought the butt of it down against the back of my skull. Before I could convey anything else to Trev, the world turned black.

"**O**W."

WAKING UP on a strange floor with your arms bound is probably never fun (this was my first time, so I couldn't really be sure, but it seemed like a safe bet). It's even less fun, however, when you have a raging headache and a goose egg on the back of your head (again, no basis for comparison, but this seemed like another obvious truth).

Embracing the whole "I'm a victim of a recent head trauma" trope, I lay there and moaned for a bit while I waited for the world to stop spinning. As the room settled into a single ceiling with only four walls, instead of the crazy-assed kaleidoscope it had started off as, I began to put my thoughts in order.

Clearly, my warning to Trevor hadn't been quite fast enough. Or, at least, it hadn't been fast enough for them to stop Algernon before he ran off with me. Hopefully, it had at least been enough to keep any of them from getting caught by whoever had Algernon by the nuts.

I decided to remain prone. Besides not feeling capable of the ab workout it would take to get upright with all of my limbs tied behind me, my head was pounding enough to make my gorge rise without putting it through the trauma of changing its elevation. So, even when I heard the unmistakable sound of a door opening to my right, I didn't bother to move much. Instead, I slowly and carefully turned my head to see who had come to torment me.

It turned out to be a pale, thin, elderly-looking man, wearing a pinstriped three-piece suit, who was dragging my uncle Algernon behind him like an unwilling rag doll in one hand and holding a gun in the other. The odd mirroring of two well-dressed older men was almost comical. The man with the gun looked like a faded version of my great-uncle, boasting less hair, less melanin, and less style.

I sighed.

"I fucking hate guns."

I hadn't meant to say it aloud, but it appeared the blow to my head had turned off my filters.

"Wretched things, aren't they?" said the man holding the object in question. He raised it and pressed it to Algernon's temple, looking for all the world as if it disgusted him to do so.

"Nonetheless, they make effective tools."

I couldn't argue with that, so I said nothing.

"I can tell from your silence that you're inclined to agree with me. It's a shame, really. I miss the days when all these things could be settled amicably simply by knowing who held the stronger magic."

"Were you alive for those days?" I asked.

The guy didn't look more than sixty or seventy, but I imagine that the days when guns *weren't* great equalizers between magic and non-magic folks had been a good long time ago.

"Sadly, no. Still, one can dream…"

"I suppose." I tried to shift a bit more onto my side, in order to relieve some of the strain in my neck, but the man turned the gun on me with surprising agility.

"Just trying to get comfortable," I said quickly, hoping to keep us from getting shot.

"Well, don't," he replied testily.

I nodded. Slowly.

"Now then, tell me where your brother is, Ms. Marmot, lest I be forced to shoot your uncle here."

He pointed the gun at Algernon again, and I tried to swallow, but there was suddenly no saliva left in my mouth.

"I don't know where he is right at the moment," I replied. The man thumbed off the safety on the gun. I would have raised my hands if I could, but since they were still tied behind me, I just kept talking. "But the last place I saw him was in my house, just before Algernon here held me at gunpoint on my own front step."

The man glared at me as though I were a level of stupid he had not yet encountered.

"I don't believe that you would be imbecilic enough to bring a known MOME fugitive to hide in your home. Surely you realize it would be the first place we would look."

That had me returning the look he'd just given me.

"Except that, if I'm correct in surmising that your whole goal in holding me here is to find out where Trevor is, then you clearly *didn't* look there. Or maybe you just weren't able to. I think my brother is easily a few steps ahead of… whatever it is you guys use for spying and eavesdropping these days."

He didn't lower the gun on Algernon and continued staring at me.

"Fine," he said, after a lengthy pause, "If you're going to play hardball, we can do that. I didn't want to have to draw this out, but you leave me no choice."

He pushed the gun into his belt, just in front of the pinstriped vest, a move that made me cringe. But my wincing at poor gun safety was cut short as he pulled a six-inch dagger from somewhere inside his vest.

Without pausing to repeat any of his questions, or even explain what he intended to do, he brought up the wrist by which he had been restraining Algernon and rammed the knife into it, all the way to the hilt. Algernon and I screamed at the same time.

"What the FUCK, dude?! I told you, my bother is in my fucking house. It's not my fault if your people are too incompetent to find him there. And it certainly isn't Algernon's fault."

I could feel tears run down my cheeks. Algernon and I had never been particularly close, but after my parents died, or disappeared, or whatever the fuck they did, he was all that I had left until I found Trevor again. We had enjoyed a few companionably silent teas, and shared enough teary hugs that I really didn't want anything bad to happen to him, not to mention that he was just a decent human being who didn't deserve to be stabbed in the wrist by a psychopath.

Mr. Pinstripe looked up at me then, even as Algernon crumpled to the floor, his arm still hanging awkwardly from the other man's grip. He glared at me, but said nothing.

"Use a fucking truth spell if you have one, or whatever you want. But that's all I know about where my brother is. He was at my fucking house when you assholes took me. If you'd done your jobs properly, he would be here right now. So STOP. TORTURING. MY. UNCLE."

"Interesting," said Mr. Pinstripe. "I hadn't expected that you had inherited any of your grandfather's gifts."

I had less than no idea what he was talking about, but as he wasn't driving any more knives into Algernon, I was going to count it as a win.

"What do you mean?"

"You just put power behind your words. I can tell because I feel inclined to stop stabbing your uncle here, which, I can guarantee you, is not my usual mode of operations."

"So, you enjoy stabbing people?" I asked, my voice carefully neutral. "Tell me more about that."

Ok, yeah, so maybe it was a cheap attempt to keep the man talking, but hell, I would play shrink all day if it meant giving my rescuers more time to find me. And yes, I assumed I had rescuers, because, well, damn it all, we had just spent the morning bro-ing it up over how we all saved each other's asses and would do it again. So, yeah, I expected my posse to be coming after me. Assuming they could find me.

It would be easy enough to tell them where I was if I had any earthly idea myself.

I had considered, very briefly, when the man was first pointing the gun at Algernon, just shifting myself away from here. But that would leave Algernon alone, with a man who was very pissed off holding a gun to his temple, and I didn't think that would end well for Algernon. So I had stayed, but if I could somehow convince Mr. Pinstripe to let me touch Algernon… maybe I wouldn't even need a rescue.

Pinstripes just sneered at me.

"I'm not a serial killer in search of validation, or a Bond villain looking for an audience, so I'm afraid your questions about my motivations will go unanswered. The organization I work for has a vested interest in your brother. That is all you need to know, I'm afraid."

He turned toward Algernon and pulled the knife rather slowly from his forearm. Algernon screamed again, and I shuddered.

Pinstripe was just raising the knife to plunge back into Algernon's arm, while I flailed futilely against the bonds holding my wrists, when the door flew open with a bang and Sol sauntered in.

"WHAT THE FUCK are you doing with my assignment, Vince?" Sol asked.

I kept my mouth shut. My body had flooded with relief at the first sight of Sol, but her words made me realize that she might not be here to rescue me. After all, she had a rep to keep with her MOME superiors. She would be risking a lot to break that cover. She was probably just here to assess the situation.

I doubted she would let Mr. Pinstripe, aka Vince, kill me if it came down to it, though. So that was somewhat reassuring.

"Just getting some useful information out of her before she's put down. Seeing as you managed to end her usefulness before it even began."

"You're not going to touch her, and neither is anyone else. I spent MONTHS tracking this bitch, and I didn't do all of that to have you ruin her before we even find out if she's useful."

Well, that was a different story than the one that Sol had been selling us earlier. I wondered how much of the change in tune was for Vince's benefit, or how much Sol had simply glossed over the truth in order to get on our good side.

"She already lost whatever usefulness she might have had when you let her thrice-cursed brother escape. She was only ever good as collateral."

"That's not what my department thinks."

Sol said that last bit with the kind of authority that implied her department was not to be fucked with.

Vince just eyed her for a moment, but before he could do anything else, she turned to Algernon.

"Who's the old man?" she asked, sneering.

"The freaks' great-uncle. He's *helping* us in return for a favor."

"Oh?" said Sol, sounding barely interested. "What favor?"

"Not killing his grandchildren."

"Hmm… they at HQ?" she asked, looking around the room, as though she were more interested in the decor than the question itself.

Vince didn't reply, and Sol just shrugged.

"Well, I have good news, Vince. I have the brother. So you can go ahead and move on with your day."

That made Vince narrow his eyes.

"Why are you telling *me* that instead of HQ?"

"Because HQ sent me over here to find out what the hell kind of shady shit you were up to, and I'm the one who found him."

"Where was he?"

Vince was toying with the knife in a way that was not at all reassuring. He looked like he was just itching to stick it back into some human flesh. Creepy. Vince was officially a creepy fuck.

"In her house," Sol said, turning back to Vince and looking smug. "Dumbest place to hide him they could have thought of. Of course, they didn't even *try* to hide him from *me*."

Apparently Vince didn't like Sol's tone, or else he decided that Sol's revelation meant that Algernon's existence was no longer useful to anyone. Whatever his motivations, he lunged forward with his knife hand. I shouted a warning, but could only watch in horror from my prone position on the floor.

Just as the knife was about to reach Algernon's throat, a giant, black ball of fury and teeth slammed Vince into the wall behind them both. Algernon whimpered and looked like he might faint, but otherwise seemed unharmed.

When Sol-as-panther stepped back from Vince, the man's head flopped vacantly to one side, a large gash having taken the place of where his Adam's apple used to reside.

"Ew," I said, feeling my gorge rise. "I mean, don't get me wrong, he deserved it, but… yuck. I never realized how gross the human trachea looks."

Algernon held a hand to his mouth and moved to the corner of the room, but he didn't quite make it before his most recent meal came up to visit.

"And, that's even more gross," I mentioned, trying to turn away, but only managing to close my eyes against the image, desperately trying not to think of the smell.

Suddenly, Sol in human form was kneeling over me, doing something with the bonds that held me.

I was surprised by how quickly my nausea fled and was replaced by a very different kind of warmth in my stomach.

"Remind me to stay on your good side," I mumbled to Sol, as she loosened the bonds on my wrists.

She just smirked and continued untying me.

"Is this going to be problematic for you… work-wise? And how did you find me?"

"I'll explain once we're safely out of here," Sol said, as she finally undid the binding around my ankles.

"Should I shift us?" I asked.

Sol shook her head, but didn't say anything, looking pointedly at Algernon, who was still being quietly sick in the corner of the room.

Interesting, and mildly suspicious, that Sol didn't want to discuss things in front of him, but I supposed one couldn't be too careful.

"Ok. What's our exit strategy, then?"

Sol strode to a window that I hadn't been able to see this whole time because of the way I'd been positioned on the floor, and flung open the blinds, then the window itself.

She whistled loudly, and there was a return howl from outside. I had already gone to kneel beside Algernon.

"Come on, Algie. We have to get out of here quickly. We need time to find your family before they have a chance to hurt them."

Algernon stared at me through glassy eyes.

"I can't leave here. They'll kill my granddaughters. I can't risk it. If you can find them, please, help them. Get them away from MOME, but I can't risk doing anything that might seem like not cooperating."

I stared at him in consternation, while gesturing vaguely in the direction of the newly deceased. "Vince over there was ready to kill you because he'd decided that you'd outlived your usefulness. What makes you think whoever else is here won't do the same?"

Algernon simply shook his head.

"That doesn't matter. I have to know that my granddaughters are safe. They can do whatever they like with me, but those girls…"

Algernon's eyes filled, and I did my best to keep from imitating him, not because I didn't think it was an appropriate time to cry, it certainly was, but because I needed clear vision to get out of here fast enough to save Algernon's grandkids.

I took a deep breath.

"Damn it, Algie, if I'd just wanted to leave you to the sharks, I would have abandoned you the second I woke up."

Sol growled softly from behind me, but I didn't bother to turn around to see if it was directed at me or not. I didn't think Algernon was with it enough to put together that I meant I could shift people through space and time, but how did MOME not already know that anyway? I had shifted the four of us out of their clutches not twenty four hours ago.

"Come with us, please. I'll make sure they can't get to the girls."

He shook his head, and Sol muttered "We have to go," so softly that I doubted anyone without enhanced hearing would be able to even tell that she'd spoken.

I sighed.

"Please be careful, Tio. I'll do my best to get Lucy and Mia away from these assholes. Your part of the deal is to make sure you're around to see them again. Ok?"

Algernon nodded, but still didn't speak. I decided I didn't have time to do anything other than run to the window and follow Sol's lead, reaching for my snow leopard and jumping out of the open frame as close to her furry tail as I could manage without landing us in a tangled heap of cat.

As we hit the ground running, I felt the getting-more-familiar-than-I-would-like flash of heat caused by a spell whizzing past my shoulder, and I began zigging and zagging my way to Seamus, whose wolf form I could just see in the distance. My hope was that the quick directional changes would help prevent spells from turning me into a gooey Picasso or… whatever they were intended to do.

I heard a screech from the sky above us that told me Trevor was close by, and I wondered how long they'd been out here fighting off mages.

Long enough that we're getting tired, Numo.

More spells burst onto the landscape nearby, and I heard Seamus howl once behind me, just as we neared the woods bordering the grounds of the estate we appeared to be on. I hadn't been able to tell much about the house we'd been inside of from my limited perspective tied up on the floor, so this was the first time I was getting any sense of the size and shape of the place.

We had jumped from a second story window and landed in a heavily landscaped garden, complete with artfully manicured lawn and oddly sculpted decorative shrubs.

Like, seriously, why had I just run past a hedge shaped like a herring? And why did I know what a herring looked like, come to that?

Within a hundred yards, however, stood the edge of a forest that I was willing to bet backed onto the nearest mountain, and might, therefore, provide us not only with cover from spells, but also an avenue of escape.

I risked a look back over my shoulder and saw that Seamus was lagging behind. Just to add to the fun, his slow pace seemed to be leaving him in serious danger of getting hit by more spells.

I turned on my haunches and sprinted back in his direction, before I could think better of it. A plaintive screech from behind me told me that Trevor had seen the move and was not impressed. Oh well. I had too few friends to risk losing any to MOME asshats. Surely, Trev of all people could understand that.

Seamus seemed similarly nonplussed when I arrived at his side, but I ignored his growl of protest, flattening him to the ground just as another spell shot towards where his head had just been.

It seemed as though the mages were catching up.

In fact, for the first time since the encounter where Trev had immolated a MOME agent in Bolivia, I could actually see who was attacking us. The spells on the cliff side had seemed like disembodied magic floating at us without an origin, since all of the mages who had been coming after us had still been on top of the cliff. And, until a few moments ago, the mages coming after us here had been behind the cover of the various decorative shrubs. Now, finally, they were forced to leave the limited protection of the oddly shaped bushes in order to cross the open ground of the estate and reach the forest beyond before we did.

I could smell the coppery tang of blood coming from Seamus, beneath me, and knew that if I hadn't just pounced on him, yet another spell would have hit him, doing who knew what kind of damage.

No time, Trevor sent, from wherever he was, flapping away behind me.

He and Sol had likely turned back to try to cover my tail as I had run for Seamus, but I wasn't sure and it wasn't like I had time to check. I needed to get Seamus out of here. Now. Injured, he wasn't fast enough for this. He needed help.

Without waiting to confirm the plan with anyone else, I thought about the clearing where the Tree of Life resided and reached for that space with my consciousness.

Between one heartbeat and the next we were there.

Seamus lay panting beneath me, but I didn't wait to see how he was doing. The Tree of Life was supposed to take care of him, and I couldn't leave Sol and Trevor in the hands of those mages, no matter how badass each of them might be normally. They were grossly outnumbered.

I shifted back to the exact place I had just left.

I felt a foot connect with my ribcage, just as I heard a human cry out in surprise, and knew that someone must have tripped over me. I could only hope that it was one of the MOME mages and not Sol or Trev.

A flash of flame to my left caught my attention and I ran towards it, desperate to get to Trevor before MOME got ahold of him.

When I reached him, he was diving repeatedly at a mage who kept shooting what looked like nets of magic at him from the end of a wand. He would dodge and attack her all in the same move, over and over again, and part of me wondered if she was just meant to be a distraction while some other mage came at him from a different angle.

Apparently, my guess was spot on. Suddenly, a second net made out of light flew towards Trevor, just as he swooped away from the first mage he'd been dodging. It looked like the second net was about to enclose him, but just before it hit him, the flames that enveloped his phoenix form flared brighter. When they faded back to their normal glow, the light net was nowhere to be seen.

I briefly wondered how many types of spells he could burn through, but then I was close enough to leap through the air and collide with the giant bird that was my brother. I didn't wait for us to land before I shifted us to the clearing with the Tree of Life.

We landed hard in the leaves and dirt that made up the clearing, and I saw that Seamus had shifted to human and was making his way towards the Tree of Life itself. I didn't wait to see how angry Trevor was with me for interfering, I shifted back to the grounds at the house.

I found Sol cornered by three mages, and I wasn't sure how to get to her without getting us both killed. She was backed into an alcove created around an impressive statuary, and she must have just arrived there, because I couldn't see a reason for the mages not to have killed her already, if they'd had the time and inclination.

Not knowing what else to do, I climbed the closest shrub and gained as much elevation as possible. When I launched myself at Sol, it was from the height of about fifteen feet, and I sailed easily over the heads of the three mages that had her pinned into that corner. Unfortunately, I wasn't faster than the mages had been at preparing their spells, and three of them hit Sol at once, just before I did. I didn't wait for the breath to return to my body after the impact of slamming into her from fifteen feet away, I just shifted us to the clearing as quickly as I could.

When we materialized in front of the Tree of Life, Sol wasn't breathing.

I SPRANG AWAY from her, my nimble snow leopard form leaping away backwards even as I pulled on the human part of me and transitioned to walking on two legs.

The lack of my weight on her chest did not make her start breathing.

I instantly fell to her side.

"LIFE!" I cried, as I knelt next to her prone, furry form. Her glossy black coat was slick with blood.

"LIFE!"

Suddenly, the towering form of the Tree of Life loomed behind me. Right now, the scythe was particularly off-putting.

"Heal her!"

IT IS TOO LATE. HER LIFE FORCE IS GONE.

"No. Damn it, Life! What good are you, if you can't save people who have only been dead for five seconds? There are regular humans who can do that!"

PERHAPS YOU SHOULD TAKE HER TO THEM, THEN.

"But she was killed by magic! I don't know what a hospital can even do for her."

Life just stared at me.

"Fuck this!"

Tears streamed down as I turned to the one person who had never failed me yet.

"Trev, please."

He looked at me like he didn't understand at first, but then, slowly, he must have realized what I was asking.

"Please," I begged, unable to let Sol die, for all that I'd only known her for a handful of days. I wasn't sure that he could truly do anything, but clung to the hope that some of the myths were true. I'd spent the past week getting a crash course in living fantasy, and damn it, if the naked lady in the woods who claimed to be my narrator turned out to actually be a goddess, the guy in my English class turned out to be a werewolf, and the guy stalking me in my fucking bedroom turned out to be a vampire, then surely this miracle was possible.

Please, please, dear Gwen, let it be possible.

Trev nodded, though he looked far from confident. He reached down and set both of his hands on Sol's prone form.

And then flames consumed her.

SEAMUS, TREV, AND I watched the flames consume Sol's body, and I struggled to remind myself that she was technically dead, so the flames weren't hurting her. But damned if it didn't look like the flames were hurting her. Her body convulsed repeatedly, and I was extremely thankful that the fire was too bright for us to make out what was being done to her flesh.

Gwen damn it, if all that was left after this was a charred corpse, I was going to feel like a first rate asshole. Not to mention, I would probably never forgive myself for having gotten Sol killed to begin with.

I felt an arm wrap around my shoulder and turned to see Seamus still staring at the flaming body on the ground, but leaning against me as though he needed the support as much as I did.

"She doesn't even like you," I said, unsure about the devastation that registered in his eyes, but mainly just saying the first words that came to mind.

One corner of his mouth turned up.

"She was raised to hate wolves. Someone in her family is an asshole, certainly, but she apologized for all that last night, when we were at the house before you and Trev got there."

"Bonded over almost dying together?" I asked. He nodded.

"You guys make out?" I asked.

"I don't think Sol's into me that way," he replied, still leaning against me, still watching the flames.

"You're using the present tense," I whispered. "You think she's still in there?"

Seamus nodded, his eyes flickering with reflected phoenix fire.

I turned back to the flames, finally letting out a deep breath I didn't know I'd been holding.

As if my breath were a gale force wind, the flames around Sol extinguished.

"Well, that was intense," said a calm, slightly accented voice, from the ground.

"Sol!?" the three of us shouted, jumping forward. I knelt at her side and grabbed her hand, doing my best to ignore the pulse of sexual heat that coursed through me at the contact.

"What the fuck just happened?" she asked.

I looked around the glade at Seamus and Trev, as if to confirm that my mind wasn't fucking with me and that I was really seeing a whole, living, distractingly naked Soledad lying on the ground in front of me.

Seamus and Trev were crying, but also laughing and smiling, so I had to assume that I wasn't hallucinating the whole thing.

"Um… the bad guys killed you, and then Trev brought you back."

I HELPED.

"And Life helped," I added, laughing and sobbing at the same time, not wanting to piss off the tree, even though he'd claimed he couldn't do anything to start with.

Sol laughed, and then sat up. I thought really hard about her being fully dressed, and was somewhat surprised to see her clothed a moment later.

"¿Qué demonios?" she asked.

"Um… I think that was my Gwen powers acting up." I carefully did not mention that I found naked Sol decidedly distracting. For one thing, I was embarrassed not to have more self-control, and for an-other, I didn't want to weird out my friends and make them think I was objectifying them.

"How did that even work?" Seamus asked, look-ing between Trev and Sol as though he expected either of them to burst into flames at any moment.

"It has never worked before," Trev said, looking both bewildered and a bit sad. "Maybe having the Tree of Life here was the difference, but… yeah. Phoenix fire is supposed to lead to rebirth, so… it was a last ditch effort."

I took a moment to be appropriately horrified that Trev had needed to try that trick before, and then another moment to mourn the fact that it hadn't worked. Then I got back to the business of being amazed at what he'd done.

"Why did you get all the cool powers?" I asked, giving him a teasing push.

"Dude, Vic, you turn into a snow leopard and can move people through time and space in the blink of an eye," he replied, leveling me with his best "srsly" face.

"Yeah, but only because a goddess decided to turn me into one of her minions. You were born with this!"

Trev shook his head.

"Sort of… there's a lot more that any of us could do. The dark matter inside each of us is more raw potential than a set of genetically predetermined 'powers.' MOME, and everyone else, have perpetuated the myth that people can't access power in ways they weren't born to, but that's a lie. Shifters can use their powers to access spells if they train the right way, and a mage could call on an animal form if they practiced hard enough. Regular humans could probably access a spell or two, if they trained enough. They have to have some amount of dark matter, or else Vampires wouldn't use them for snacks."

And in that one statement, Trev had told me more about the magical world than I'd learned in the past week. I looked to Seamus and Sol for confirmation, but they both had their eyebrows pinned to their hairlines as though Trev had just claimed that vivisecting puppies was a good time.

"Trev, why do Seamus and Sol look like you just kicked them in the face?"

"Probably because no one in our world wants to talk about how similar shifters and mages are, and how our powers are the same at the root."

"And why do you know so much about this taboo subject?" I prodded.

"It's what MOME was training me in, before I escaped."

"And it's the reason we really shouldn't be discussing things here," said a vaguely familiar British voice from the edge of the clearing. I wrinkled my nose at the cloying smell of weed and realized who it must be.

"Mr. Bumblebee?" I asked, turning towards the voice.

"Please, Victoria, I believe I asked you to call me Albert."

"Yes. Sorry, Albert. It's been… a long few days since then."

"Vic?" Trev asked, looking as though he was ready to attack the newcomer at any moment. Indeed, Sol had already jumped to her feet, and she and Seamus both looked ready to fight as well.

"Um… team, this is Albert Bumblebee. He knew my parents."

I had made a split second decision that I didn't necessarily want Albert to know who Trevor was, assuming he didn't already, so I didn't bother to explain that my parents were also Trev's.

You don't trust him? Trev asked, having noticed the exclusion.

I don't know. Maybe? It's hard to say. He hasn't given me reason not to, but… where MOME is concerned, can we really trust anyone?

Fair point.

"It's only a matter of time until MOME decides to try their luck here. I'm afraid the Tree of Life isn't entirely a secret."

"Vic, can you take us somewhere?" Seamus asked. I could tell that he was doing his best not to share too much about my newfound powers with Albert, but I was at a loss as to how we were going to keep him from finding out as soon as I actually shifted in front of him.

"I think I've got enough energy for one more shift, thanks to Life here, but where do we go? We can't go to my place, that's the first place they'll look now."

"We could try my place," Seamus suggested, but I was shaking my head as soon as he'd said it.

"Too risky. They've probably figured out who you are by now. It's not worth putting your family at risk. We should probably get out of the state if we can."

Sol sighed.

"You know where to take us, Gatita."

I looked at her. She had a point. Assuming that MOME hadn't somehow discovered her cabin since the last time we were there—which didn't seem at all likely, since they'd only discovered that she was working against them in the past half hour or so—I stepped forward and grabbed Sol and Trevor's hands. Seamus took Sol's other hand, and I focused on a mental image of Sol's little wood cabin on a Bolivian mountainside, willing us all to be there instead of here, even as the image came into focus in my mind.

Then an arm wrapped around my chest, and I heard Albert shout, "Damn it all, how did he find us!"

The world went black.

WHEN I OPENED my eyes, we stood on the side of a mountain in a blizzard so thick that I could barely see the small log cabin that stood less than a meter away. Yet I ignored the slashing cold that battered me, as well as the warmth that lay within easy reach, and instead focused on beating the ever-living crap out of the creepy, undead dickwad who had his arm around my chest.

"Victoria, wait!" Edik shouted.

I did not wait. I pulled on my snow leopard form and set about inserting my three-inch claws into his undead flesh.

"Aghhhhhh!!! Victoria, stop!"

Spoiler alert—I didn't stop.

I was so fucking sick of Edik showing up in my life and screwing things up. In particular, I was sick of him touching me as though he had any right to do so, in any way, ever. A rage coursed through me that I hadn't known I was capable of as I slashed at him again and again, slicing through the flesh of the forearms he feebly held in front of his face as protection.

I roared, my whole feline body shaking with fury, and slashed at him again and again.

"Victoria, please! I'm only seeking my daughter."

And what did I care if that was true? His daughter probably never wanted to see him again. She probably hated him with every fiber of her being. Maybe she wanted him dead.

Maybe I was projecting…

That last thought didn't occur to me until multiple sets of arms worked to restrain me, and Trev whispered into my furry ear, "It's ok, Vic. We won't let him touch you again. Maybe let him live. Just for a minute…"

I snarled, and did my best to take another swipe at Edik, but Sol's arms were wrapped around my shoulders, holding my front legs against me, and I couldn't get at him without possibly slicing her up, which I wasn't willing to do.

I shifted back to human form, fully clothed thanks to Gwen's bonus powers, and without saying a word, I turned, brushing three sets of arms away from me, and strode into the cabin.

As soon as I stepped inside my legs gave out from under me.

~~~

"You've overtaxed your magical reserves," said a British accent that I was beginning to recognize.

"What is Albert doing here?" I asked the room, which was still spinning above me.

"He hitched a ride along with Sir Sparkle Brains," Trev muttered.

"I only hitched a ride *because* of Sir Sparkle Brains, as you call him. You'd made it clear enough that you didn't wish to have me with you, but when I saw him latch onto Victoria, I thought I would offer my services at vampire disabling."

I couldn't see Albert, because I was too busy trying to get the ceiling to stop rotating.

"Well, you do seem to have a knack for it," Seamus admitted from somewhere by my feet.

"Where *is* Mr. McStabbyTeeth?" I asked.

"He's outside in the snow, looking for all the world like a miniature statue of David." That was Sol.
~~~

"Huh?" My brain really wasn't up to the task of well… probably even basic addition at this point, let alone trying to unravel references to Italian statuary and biblical figures.

"Albert froze him or something, and he's pale enough that he kind of looks like marble anyway. He's out there collecting snow," Trevor's voice added.

"Not that he doesn't deserve to freeze to death, but… I assume that he won't?" I asked.

"Nope. Unfortunately, vamps don't need warmth to survive," Sol replied, sounding truly disappointed.

I blinked, unsure if I was relieved or disappointed at the news that he would survive the cold. Unable to make up my mind, I took a moment to appreciate that the ceiling was now mostly stationary.

"So, how long before I can shift us again?" I asked.

For a long moment no one replied. Or maybe I fell asleep briefly, it was hard to tell.

"Probably not for a day or two. It depends on how much you've been practicing."

That was Albert's voice again, and I still couldn't convince my head to turn and look at anyone, so I didn't have the benefit of facial expressions to help me figure out if that was meant to be an admonishment or not.

"Considering that I've only had most of these powers for a day or two, it is safe to say I've hardly practiced at all. If it weren't for the Tree of Life I'd probably be dead already. Twice."

Albert began to object, although whether he was going to protest the idea that I'd only had magic for two days, or the fact that the Tree of Life had saved me twice already, I didn't know, because Sol cut him off.

"You need rest, regardless," Sol said, and it sounded like she was fussing with the wood stove while she spoke. "MOME doesn't know about this. So as long as Edik and Gramps here don't turn us in, we should be safe while you rest up."

"And what do we do with Edik?" I asked. "Leave him sitting outside like a statue?"

Sol chuckled. "Sure. The cabin could use some decoration. We can have Albert unfreeze him once you're rested enough to shift us all away if he pulls anything sketchy."

That sounded like as good a plan as any, and before anyone had a chance to suggest an alternative, I fell into a deep sleep.

I WOKE UP to a deep thrum that reverber-
ated all the way down my spine. Not wanting
to do anything that might make that pleasant
feeling stop, I waited a few minutes before opening
my eyes. After a few blissful minutes of just listening, I felt sufficiently awake to realize that the
sound was that of an upright bass being bowed. Or
at least that was my best guess, since I'd noticed an
upright bass in Sol's cabin before, hadn't seen any
other string instruments lying around, and knew
that whatever it was, it sounded like nothing I'd
heard before. I opened my eyes and the sound
stopped.

"Don't," I said, sitting up and turning towards
the corner of the room, where I found Sol still holding the upright against her with one arm, her other
hand loosely holding the bow at her side.

"Sorry," she said. "After you slept through all the shouting, I didn't think this would wake you up."

"Please don't stop," I said, before my brain could process the fact that Sol had mentioned shouting.

She started playing again before I could ask, and I didn't stop her. The sound was entirely too pleasant, and watching her play turned out to be even more pleasant. She was wearing a T-shirt and jeans, since the wood stove was kicking out maximum heat, and the muscles of her arms as she fingered the strings and drew the bow across them was hypnotizing. Damn it. I was going to have to go jump in a snowbank or something. I stood up, suddenly conscious of how turned on I was, and decided it might be a good idea to let my cat out.

Saying nothing, because *Sorry, Sol, I can't stay and watch you play because it's making me want to tear all of your clothes off and I feel that would be disrespectful of both you and the music* wasn't high on my list of things to say to other humans (if I didn't already have permission to tear the clothes off of them periodically), I walked out the small wooden door that led to mountainside beyond and thought about being a snow leopard until it went from memory to reality.

Running over and around snow, rocks, trees, and the occasional cliff was exhilarating and refreshing in a way that nothing else was. I felt free, and truly myself as I never did as a human. It was as though all of the backpacking, trail running, and rock climbing I had ever done had all been a pathetic attempt to achieve the true freedom of being a giant, mountain-climbing cat. I may have let out a few celebratory yowls. Perhaps a feline barbaric yawp.

I didn't run for very long. Just enough to take care of some basic needs out of sight of the house and raise my respiratory rate a bit. I could cover so much ground in so little time in this form that I probably went for what my human form would have found to be a three hour hike, but I ran it in a handful of minutes. The terrain here was a bit gentler than a snow leopard was designed for and, as I headed back to the house, I suddenly had a very strong desire to travel to the Himalayas.

Ha! That was probably gonna have to wait.

I shifted back to my human form as I neared the tiny log cabin that was nestled on what was probably the only remotely level bit of mountainside for miles. I took a moment to once again appreciate that something about Gwen's transfer of power made it so that I was always appropriately clothed in my human form. I was now wearing a pair of fleece lined jeans over long underwear and a soft cashmere sweater with a down vest over it. It wasn't warm enough to linger on the mountainside for long, but it was perfect for the wood stove heated cabin, and adding a parka and some snow pants would make it a solid base for the Andes in springtime. I had no idea where the clothes had come from, but whoever had dressed me, I couldn't fault their taste.

Ignoring Edik's frozen form, doing my best not to look at his slightly anguished eyes, and feeling rather proud that I had managed to resist the urge to pee on him so far, I walked inside.

"Sorry," I said to Sol, as I walked to the wood stove and moved the still-full kettle onto one of the burners there. She still had her head bent over the bass. "Had to pee," I added.

She smiled and looked up from the bass, and when her yellow eyes caught mine my heart almost stopped.

"No worries, Gatita. You'd been asleep for a while."

Which reminded me of her earlier statement and distracted me from the heat spreading through my body simply from having locked eyes with her. What the hell was up with that? "You said I slept through some shouting?"

She nodded and, finishing the last bar of whatever melody she was playing, sheathed her bow in its holster on the side of the instrument and leaned the massive thing against the wall in the corner after collapsing the foot.

"Albert and Trevor were getting into it over something. Not sure what, though. I think it had to do with your parents."

Well, that was interesting.

"You didn't hear any details?" I asked. That seemed weird, if they had been shouting.

"I heard everything, but I couldn't understand most of it. Not sure what language it was, but it wasn't English or Spanish."

"Huh. Weird. Not sure what other language Trev speaks aside from Tibetan, but why would Albert speak Tibetan?"

"Hmmm… could have been Tibetan. I didn't think of that, but I should have, considering the file I was given on you before my assignment. I knew your mom's family was from Tibet. Anyway, it all started after they looked through that file you grabbed at MOME."

"Which is why you assume it was about my parents," I muttered, wondering what that file said. I hadn't had a chance to look at it since stealing it out of the office in MOME, due to subsequently getting shoved into a pitch black dungeon, then participating in a daring escape, then getting kidnapped, then escaping again, and then almost beating a vampire to death and collapsing in a pseudo-coma… it had been a busy two days.

Seemingly reading my thoughts, Sol picked up one of the brightly colored cushions on the couch nearest where she had been playing, then produced a manila folder from underneath it.

"Here," she said, handing it to me. "Thought you'd want to see it as soon as you could. Maybe figure out what the hell they were on about before they come back."

"Where did they go, anyway?"

"Not sure. I kicked them out when they were being too damned loud and I thought they might wake you up. Seamus went off to water some trees not long before you woke up. The other two haven't been gone an hour yet."

I nodded absently at her answer as I stared at the manila folder in front of me, hesitating to actually open it. Would it carry any answers about my parents' disappearance? Would it just confirm my newly budding suspicion that my parents were people I didn't really know?

I think that was my biggest fear, really. I'd already been shocked as hell to find out that I was a snow leopard, and that my parents were a part of the world in which that was a normal thing to be… and yet, they had never told me any of it. As cool as it was to find out you can turn into a giant, badass feline, I did feel marginally betrayed on that front… and I couldn't help but wonder if this folder would tell me a hundred more ways in which my parents weren't the people I'd always thought they were. Was that why Trevor and Albert had been yelling?

Oh well, sitting here staring at the damned thing wasn't going to get me anywhere, and wondering was worse than knowing one way or the other, that was for damned sure. So, I took a deep breath and flicked open the folder.

It took me a moment to adjust to the layout of the forms, as well as the fact that everything was in Spanish, but soon enough I was skimming the file efficiently enough to catch things that stood out. Probably the first thing that caught my eye was the fact that my last name was apparently NOT Marmot.

Ok. That really shouldn't have been too surprising considering what I now knew about my parents and their attempts to hide me from MOME, but… damn it. Was anything I "knew" about my life the truth? Ok. Fine. So, apparently my mom's last name was Milarepa… that was odd, that was a dude my mom used to tell stories about all the time when I was a kid but… ok… and now I was suddenly remembering a grandmother I'd completely forgotten about…. I could feel another headache coming on, and I wondered how much of my life had been erased by my parents' attempts to protect me.

Dad's last name had been McMarten. Boring. Still, according to our file here, my real last name was McMarten Milarepa. Well, bonus points to Mom for keeping her name, but that was a hell of a mouthful.

"I think I'll keep Marmot," I muttered, drawing a slight chuckle from the kitchen, where Sol had taken up the tea-making efforts I had abandoned after she'd distracted me with this manila bundle of angst.

Not liking the pressure that was building up beneath my temples, I shifted quickly to snow leopard and then back to human. It worked, much as it had when I'd first found out about Trev. I came back to my human form with a clearer mind and no pain.

Feeling a bit overwhelmed by the whole new last name thing, not to mention vivid images of a shriveled, tiny woman with white hair and fierce, glowing eyes, I decided to refocus my efforts on the rest of the file. The next gut punch was less personal, but still pretty sharp, and explained, in my mind, why Trev and Albert had been shouting.

"Well, shit," I muttered.

"What'd you find?" Sol asked.

"Albert used to work for MOME," I said.

"What? Why was that in your parent's file?"

"Because he was their instructor."

"Instructor for what?" she asked.

Before I could reply with the "fucked if I know" that rested on my tongue, we heard shouts just outside the door to the cabin.

We both rushed towards the door, but it burst open before we got there. Seamus stood outside, looking out of breath and wide-eyed.

"The fucking vampire is loose," he said, before collapsing to the floor.

HAVING QUICKLY DETERMINED that Seamus' maladies were likely altitude-based rather than injury-based, I left him to Sol's ministrations, rushing out through the door to discover Edik running faster than my eyes could easily track between the low trees and boulders that surrounded the cabin, dodging the spells that Albert was firing at him, and all the while shouting his innocence.

"I'm just searching for my daughter!" he cried, diving behind a large rock as yet another burst of… something nasty looking… shot from Albert's extended hands.

"Yes, yes. So you've said," Albert replied calmly, as though they were having a peaceful conversation in which Albert wasn't trying to kill him. "But we really can't have you running off to tell MOME where we are, can we? If you would just hold still. I'm only trying to restrain you."

Huh. Whatever Albert was flinging at Edik looked like it was meant to do more than restrain, but hell, what did I know?Maybe the fact that it obliterated rock didn't mean it would obliterate vampire… diamond skulls, and all that.

"MOME doesn't have Renata, so I don't have the slightest interest in helping them! You all know where she is! You must!"

He was forced to break in his pleading to dive behind yet another boulder, with Albert's spell missing him by mere inches.

I couldn't help but think that Albert was one to talk when it came to snitching us out to MOME, but as I had absolutely zero love for Edik, I didn't mention it. Trev sat on a rock nearby, seeming completely unconcerned with the proceedings.

Did you find out what Albert was teaching our parents? I asked, since Albert seemed to have Edik distracted. I was more concerned with the possible threat that Albert posed than whatever bullshit Edik was spewing this time.

Trev raised an eyebrow in an expression visible even from twenty feet away.

You know about that? he asked.

I was just reading their file before Lord Sparkle Fang started stirring up trouble.

Albert was training them much in the same way that MOME was training me these past few years. His insistence that it wasn't for nefarious purposes was what started the shouting match. Sorry if we woke you.

Does Albert speak Tibetan? I asked.

Yes. Which isn't reassuring.

Why not?

Because it's a bit of a coincidence isn't it? That he speaks Tibetan when almost no one does. It's not exactly a useful world language.

Does it have any magical uses? I asked.

Trev's face turned carefully neutral, which worried me.

It might, he said. And I wasn't sure if his hesitation was because he thought it unlikely, or because he knew more than he was willing to share.

Pretty sure I don't like you hiding shit from me, I thought to Trevor just as I stepped towards where Albert was slowly blasting away at the last boulder that Edik had disappeared behind.

"Is that not a waste of your energy?" I asked, looking between him and the large chunks of boulder that were cascading to the ground, even as Edik whimpered audibly on the other side.

"That depends on your definition of waste," Albert said, raising one side of his mouth in a decidedly non-cordial smirk. "Is it likely to help us capture him? No. Is it incredibly satisfying after years of putting up with his horse shite?"

He turned and continued to fire wave after wave of… whatever it was at the boulder and Edik.

It may make me a bad person, but I laughed. Edik really was an asshat, and after having dealt with him for less than a week I couldn't blame Albert for wanting to take potshots at him. I can't imagine how I would feel if I'd known him for years.

"Edik," I shouted, over the sounds of spells slamming into rock and sending bits crumbling to the ground. "If you'd like Albert to give up on this whole blowing you to tiny bits thing, you could just agree to be restrained and answer a few questions."

"How do I know you won't just try to kill me as soon as you have me restrained?" he shouted from behind the boulder, without showing himself.

"Maybe because we have better things to do with our time?" I suggested.

Albert scoffed. "I don't," he muttered.

"Ok, fine. Maybe because you were frozen out here for a day already and no one killed you yet."

"How do I know you won't kill me as soon as you have whatever information you want?"

I looked to Albert, and then to Trev.

"I guess you don't," I replied after a while. "But you know that Albert's perfectly willing to kill you if you do anything that makes him think you're not cooperating, so why not give cooperating a try and see if it makes him feel a bit less homicidal, or vampicidal, or whatever?"

Hmm… this whole fantasy world within my normal world was going to need a vocabulary adjustment.

"Is there a Latin root for vampire?" I muttered, to no one in particular, while Edik was silent on the other side of the rock.

"Fine. I'll talk."

Edik stepped out from behind the boulder, but before he'd even gotten a full step away from it Albert blasted him with a spell that sent him careening into the granite behind him.

"Oh. Terribly sorry. Must have slipped!" Albert almost sang, stepping forward to restrain a nearly unconscious Edik.

I couldn't decide if I wanted to laugh, or if I felt bad for Edik. If he'd been someone who hadn't just spent the past few nights terrorizing me in my own home, I would certainly have leaned towards the latter, but as it was…

"Oops," I said. "Well, Edik, you can hope that Albert has had his fun for the afternoon. In the meantime, we need to know what in the seven hells you're doing here."

As I spoke, Edik's form became wrapped in some creepy tendril things that must have been under Albert's control, because they certainly didn't seem to be making any effort to be gentle with their captive. Edik still looked disturbingly handsome, despite being covered in dirt and flecks of granite. I kinda hated how he remained so aesthetically pleasing despite being such a complete and utter douchetart.

"I already told you. I am searching for my daughter," Edik grunted, as the vine-like things that held him tightened their grip unnecessarily.

"Right. And why on earth do you think we know where she is?" I asked.

"Because she disappeared from MOME on the day that you and your friends destroyed the place. You must know where everyone went!"

Huh... I turned to look at Trevor, who was still perched on a boulder a few meters behind us. It had been his plan, his friends, his nemesis. His escape route...

"I might have some idea where most of the younger MOME detainees were headed, but I have no idea if your daughter is among them, or whether she'll want to see you, if she is."

I smiled. I was glad that was out in the open. It was difficult to imagine anyone being happy to see Edik, even his own daughter. Especially his own daughter, if what the mysterious B had said about him the other day had been true. It seemed as though B and Renata had gone through quite a bit of trouble to get away from Edik in the first place, and I wasn't sure how I felt about helping him find her again. Maybe he was an abusive piece of trash. No, scratch that, he most definitely *was* an abusive piece of trash. The question was whether or not he was an abusive piece of trash with her.

"I'm her father," Edik pleaded.

"I don't care if you created her single-handedly from a piece of clay," I replied. "If she doesn't want to see you, that's it. We will make damned sure that she isn't subjected to your presence."

"But the law—"

"I don't give a flying fuck what the law says, Edik. MOME, human, whatever. No law that forces children into the presence of their abusers gets any support from me."

"I would never hurt her." Edik's tone was the most sincere I'd ever heard from him, but that didn't change the fact that someone who thought that personal boundaries didn't matter, just because he liked someone, probably didn't have a very healthy definition of "hurt."

"There's more than one way to hurt someone, Edik. If she doesn't want to see you, she won't see you. Period. If you can't accept that, then we aren't taking you anywhere near her."

Edik nodded, though the way the blood vessels in his neck were bulging didn't leave me feeling very confident about his willingness to comply. Whatever. I could flash Renata halfway across the world in the blink of an eye if I needed to.

"Whadya, think Trev? Should we take Mr. Sparkle Fang with us?"

Trev shrugged.

"I'd rather not, but... I suppose we probably shouldn't abandon him here in the wilderness, especially with MOME HQ only a few hours' hike away..."

I thought about that for a good minute before agreeing.

"Fine. Pack your shit."

SHIT STARTED TO go wrong the second we hit the streets of Unterberg, but I was too busy being blown away by the scenery to really take notice at first.

The place was like something out of every epic fantasy book I'd ever read. Buildings that resembled the secret love-children of Notre Dame Cathedral and a drippy sandcastle were everywhere, and the streets were crammed with creatures I'd only ever seen in my imagination, along with a few that I'd never run into even there. The whole place was surrounded by steep cliffs that rose into the sky, leaving only a small strip of blue visible above. It made me wonder if we were actually underground rather than just nestled into a canyon.

Sol and Albert had given us a brief rundown on the city before we left, but it hadn't come anywhere close to doing the place justice. They'd described it as a holdout for beings that MOME considered "too dangerous," along with anyone else that managed to piss MOME off, and, as it technically wasn't located on earth, MOME held no sway there. That, and they weren't allowed in the "door," as it were. This small dimensional pocket, which could be accessed from numerous places around the world, but was only about the size of New York City, was ruled by a committee of elected members, all of whom had an equal vote in determining the few laws they bothered to uphold, the most stringent of which was that MOME agents were not allowed within its perimeter for any reason. That was the bare bones explanation we got before we arrived, and it had made me stare at Sol quizzically before she'd shrugged and explained that her Abuela had worked out some sort of deal with Unterberg ages ago and her arrival wouldn't cause a stir.

Even as we wandered down a cobbled street packed with creatures of every description, and some that defied words, I was still unclear on how we'd gotten here, since we hadn't really used my powers to do it. I'd transported us to a sketchy-looking alleyway in La Paz that Sol had shown me photos of and described in detail, a shift that had tired me out substantially, since I'd moved so many of us to a place I'd never been before, and then Albert had used some spell or other to light up a brick wall, which we all then proceeded to walk through as if it were no more than a tepid waterfall. On the other side, we'd been instantly immersed in the busy crowds of a street unlike any I'd ever seen before. I wanted to spend a few months wandering these small, winding, cobbled streets, getting lost, asking strangers for directions, and making friends with some of the amazing people I saw.

I definitely did not want to start a fistfight in the middle of the street.

But guess which of those two things I was now doing?

Yep.

My luck is shit.

The hand that clamped itself across my mouth was cold and calloused, but I didn't wait to absorb any more details about it before I threw my elbow hard into the sternum of the person attached to it. It was a good thing my backpack was nearly empty, or whoever it was might have been out of reach of my elbow, but as it was, I'd only brought along my parents' MOME file and a few essentials, so I connected solidly with whoever had tried to grab me. My heel automatically stepped back on the instep of my attacker and I heard the person cry out before stumbling away from me.

This way, Trev thought at me, as I felt his hand grab mine, and before I could even figure out how Seamus and Sol were faring, or who we were even fighting, Trev and I were running through the densely crowded street, away from Seamus, Sol, Edik, and Albert, and towards… well, I had no idea.

Where are we going? I asked mentally, since I didn't have the breath for speech.

This telepathy thing was seriously handy.

I have no idea, Trev replied. *Just trying to lead those MOME asshats on a wild goose chase.*

Those were MOME agents? I was amazed that Trev had been able to tell who had attacked us at all, since I hadn't had a chance to get a look at anyone before we'd taken off running. *How could you even tell?*

I recognized the guy who grabbed you.

It sounded like Trev was leaving something out, but I didn't have time to press the issue as our mad dash through the streets seemed to be gaining us some attention, and not just from the three (yes, I'd managed one quick look over my shoulder to count) MOME agents chasing us.

Trev's plan, whatever it was, seemed to be working, and we had MOME hot on our tails, even as we ran past carts filled with fruits and vegetables, and a few hot dishes that smelled amazing. The crowd was slowing down the MOME agents, but they weren't giving up. Unfortunately, we also had a number of large, menacing creatures forming a tight line across the street ahead of us, with the rest of the pedestrians who had been filling the streets around us somehow disappearing from view.

Who are they?

Unterberg enforcers, Trev replied.

Friendly? I asked, even as I wondered how he knew anything about what was happening, since he'd claimed never to have been here before.

Not exactly.

Trev turned left so suddenly that I probably would have lost him if I hadn't spent the first eight years of my life running around with him. Ok fine, the fact that he was still holding my hand didn't hurt.

We snapped into a narrow alleyway between two of the palatial drizzle castles that passed for buildings in this city, complete with creepy-assed gargoyle things that stared at us from the crenelated wall that demarcated each property line. The alley didn't look like a dead end, so I assumed that Trev had planned for us to make our escape that way, although how he had any idea where said alley went was beyond me. His plans seemed unlikely to matter, though.

The alley was blocked by a cadre of more of the same menacing creatures that had created a blockade across the street we'd been running through earlier. Now that I had a moment to inspect them more closely, I saw that the creatures were identical masses of what appeared to be roughly shaped clay. They had been molded into more or less human forms, but without any regard for the details.

"Are those golems?" I asked aloud, since we had stopped cold just before we'd run headlong into the oddly shaped creatures that towered before us.

"More or less," Trev assented, still panting from our run.

"Are they going to kill us?" I asked, as the creatures stepped forward in disturbing unison.

Before he could answer, a shout from behind alerted us to the MOME agents careening around the corner of the alley, with their hands readied to throw who knew what at us. I was a heartbeat away from shifting us back to Sol's cabin, when something huge and rough clamped on my shoulder and everything went black.

"**O**UCH! FUCK. THAT was unnecessary."

I would have rubbed the sore spot on my ass where I'd just been dropped onto a rock-hard surface from golem shoulder height, but my hands were tied in front of me and I couldn't even see what I'd been dropped onto, thanks to the bag that had been tied over my head.

"As is your profanity," said a lilting voice, tinged with an accent I couldn't place.

"No more than your condescending tone and mistreatment of prisoners," I replied.

"Profanity is the mark of the uneducated," said another voice, this one harsher and with a thicker accent that I still couldn't place.

"Ok, Fuckface, tell that to my dad, who had two PhDs and cursed more than anyone I know."

That was followed by a rather drawn-out silence.

It might have been awkward if I'd been able to see, but as I still had a bag on my head…

"What? Too soon?" I snickered, knowing full well that no one here had any right to be more upset about references to my possibly dead father than I did.

I had started cursing way more after my parents had died. It wasn't like I'd started cursing more on purpose, but… I don't know. Maybe it was in memory of my dad, or maybe it was just because I was a bit prickly about becoming an orphan. Algernon had pointed it out a month or two ago, and I had realized he was right, but had made no attempt to correct it.

"Perhaps it should be a privilege earned by those with more experience," said the first voice.

"Perhaps you should keep your bullshit opinions to yourself and quit policing people's use of language so damned much. If you dislike my profanity to such a degree, perhaps you should remove yourself from my presence and return to whatever prudish origins begat you. Then your knavery might entertain those more inclined to partake in it, and the rest of us might be free of your stodgy presence."

"Or you could just fuck off," added Trev's voice, from somewhere nearby.

I couldn't help it, I chuckled.

"Damn it, Trev, I was trying to keep a straight face."

"Enough of this, remove their hoods," the first, more lilting, voice said.

And with that, I was doused in light, as the bag was pulled swiftly from my head. It took a few moments of blinking to bring the room into focus, but when it did, I let out a low whistle.

The entire floor appeared to be made of a dark marble, veined with silver and gold, polished to a high shine, and reflecting the light emanating from hundreds of glowing orbs that hovered at various heights around the ornately decorated walls, all the way up to the top of a vaulted ceiling that looked like the forgotten love child of a three-year-old's sandcastle and Notre Dame cathedral.

"Nice digs," I said, deciding to embrace the sass I'd been rocking so hard, even though I was clearly (now that I could fucking *see*) talking to the rulers of Unterberg. They were all seated around the most intense conference table ever built: a foot-thick marble slab over forty feet in diameter, which appeared to be engraved with glowing runes all around the edges. "Which one of you is compensating?"

That made Trev snort, and I took a moment to look over at him for the first time since we'd been dumped here. He was lying on his side, not having bothered to sit up yet, and he had four menacing looking golems standing directly behind him.

The room we had been dumped in was larger than a football field, but one curved wall was almost directly behind us, and a series of windows appeared to open onto a giant balustrade immediately behind the twenty or so people seated around the massive piece of rock. As impressive as the rock was, it was nothing compared to the array of people seated around it. A few of them looked like elves straight out of a video game, complete with skin tones taken directly from a tipped over Crayola box. Others looked like they might spend their free time lurking under bridges with clubs, while still others looked liked they'd hopped out of Hamilton's *Mythology*. A few more had fur, wings, and horns in arrangements that I would never have predicted, despite a lifetime of reading fantasy and mythology on the daily. One or two wore hooded capes that kept them hidden from sight. None of them looked particularly "human" from where I sat, but far be it from me to deny anyone that label if they want it, so they were all people until they asked me to call them something else.

This whole scene definitely would have qualified as intimidating twenty minutes ago—ok, if I was totally honest, it was still intimidating now—but… in for a penny, in for a pound. It would seem completely two-faced to start being polite at this point and, besides, getting snatched up by golems and dumped on my ass on a marble floor with my head wrapped up in a blanket and then talked down to wasn't exactly on my list of "ways to treat me that will earn my respect" so I was just going to hold my ground and hope that it didn't get us killed.

"You do not seem to understand who you are dealing with," said the first voice that had spoken to me, which I was now able to match to an extremely tall woman who could be described as… reedy. She was even a pleasant green color, with straw-yellow hair and ears that reached delicate points well above her head.

I interrupted her as she was taking a breath to continue.

"Well, my first guess was a World of Warcraft guild meeting, but, even though your ears might back up my initial impression, I'm guessing that you're actually the folks in charge of this little realm."

I could see a few people bristle at the claim that this was a little realm, but damn, people, I had been told it was the size of New York City. Even if it matched the population of New York City, it was still "little" in the grand scheme of things.

"Geographically little, I mean. I'm sure you guys are very big where it counts," I said, through the firmest smile I could manage.

"Vic, you are totally gonna get us killed," Trev chuckled, from his spot on the floor. If he really meant that, I wondered why he was laughing.

"Well, you're no help. You must know more about these folks than I do—any sage advice is quite welcome."

Neither of us bothered dropping our voices. These folks had home court advantage, and it seemed ridiculous to assume that they couldn't hear us, no matter what we did, so there was no point in pretending. If we'd really wanted privacy, we could have spoken telepathically, but Trev hadn't bothered with that since we'd arrived, so I assumed it was either a bad idea, or simply pointless.

"Can we get to the point already? We are wasting time."

That was from the second voice that had spoken when we'd had the hoods on, which I could now see emanated from a person who looked… well, like a minotaur. I mean, a pretty handsome minotaur if such a thing were possible, but he totally had a massive, fur-covered upper body that looked quite muscular, as well as mostly human, although it was definitely holding up a bull's head, or something kind of like a bull's head. Definitely sporting a snout and horns at any rate. Kinda reinforced the whole World of Warcraft vibe, if I was being totally honest. I looked around briefly to see if anyone had snakes for hair, but no one seemed to.

"Yes, please," I replied, once I'd wrapped my mind around addressing a minotaur, "getting to the point would be great. I like you, sir. What's your name?"

Everyone just stared at me for a moment, and then the minotaur, or whatever he was, grunted.

"Torrence."

"Seriously?"

He glared at me.

"Okay… well, Torrence, let's get to the Gwen-damned point, shall we? Why have you brought us here?"

"You have brought MOME agents into our inner sanctum and you DARE question why we have brought you here?"

"We didn't bring any MOME agents wi—"

"Silence!" That was the elf lady with the seriously long ears, and she must have put a little something extra behind the words, because my mouth slammed shut before I could even think about it.

"MOME agents arrived here at the same instant you did. Whether they were chasing you or helping you is none of our concern. They are here because of you, and their presence is even less welcome than yours."

"So, the fact that we were doing everything we could to avoid MOME counts for nothing? It's all about consequences, and intentions be damned?"

"The road to hell is—"

"Oh please, don't cliche us to death. Is that the punishment for bringing MOME agents here? What's next? Pun-nishment?" I waited a beat, and Trev was kind enough to fill in with a verbal drum-roll. The rest of the room was silent.

"Tough crowd. Look, we didn't mean to bring MOME here. We will happily do all we can to help you rid yourselves of MOME in exchange for some help tracking down a friend of ours and—"

"You are in no position to negotiate," said the minotaur.

"Torrence, I thought we were friends. Look, I don't—"

"As it is your first offense," Elf Lady continued, as if I had never spoken, "you are sentenced to ten years imprisonment in the dungeon of Regnadevarg, with an option for parole at three and six years if you behave—"

"You will releasssse them to me."

My head snapped to the nearest archway in time to see Rhelia, in all her ebon-skinned, reptilian-eyed glory waltz through it, as though no one would dare stop her. Since she was a good head shorter than I was, I found that particularly impressive. I couldn't help but notice the way Trev's eyes lit up when she walked into the room, and I made a mental note to ask him about it later.

"Lady Rhelia, this sentencing hearing is not open to the public. As you are not a family member of the accused, you must—"

"He issss my *mate*," Rhelia said, pointing a regal finger at none other than my twin brother.

"WELL, THIS IS awkward," I said into the absolute silence that greeted that announcement. It had gone on long enough to make me wonder what kind of crazy taboo there was against Rhelia dating my brother. However, as I took in the shocked look that Trevor was working hard to hide, I decided that there was more going on here than Rhelia announcing that she and Trev were an item.

"I'm assuming that means she wins?"

I looked between Rhelia, Trev, and the twenty or so flabbergasted people who ran Unterberg.

Once again ignoring me as though I weren't even there, Elf Lady spoke directly to Rhelia.

"We cannot hold a dragon's kin without their express permission," she said, and then she turned to

Trev. "Do you consent to being held in the dungeon of Regnadevarg?"

Trev cleared his throat briefly, and looked like he was trying very hard not to look at Rhelia.

"I do not."

Then Elf Lady turned to me, and I had to assume that if Trev was somehow Rhelia's family, that made me family by extension, because she repeated the question.

"I do not," I replied.

"Then you are free to leave, under the protection of your dragon kin."

Trev stood up, and I moved to where he and Rhelia were now holding hands close to the door.

"Know that if you are ever found here without the protection of your dragon kin, your stay of sentencing will be revoked and—"

Rhelia whipped around to snarl at the woman, who was not only twice her height, but had the command of a massive golem army, "He issss my *mate*, Nethia. Not even death will ssssever that bond. You have no hold over *my* family!"

Nethia (up to now known as Elf Lady) fell silent, and the rest of the room began to murmur quietly.

Rhelia turned on her heel again, marching from the room. Trev and I hurried to follow.

Dare I ask what the fuck just happened? I sent to Trev.

"I will explain it shortly, Living Cat."

"Damn. I really need to work on not broadcasting to the whole damned room."

"Yessss, you do. But even sssstill you cannot hide your thoughtsss from me."

"Well, that's discouraging," I muttered.

"It's kind of her specialty, Vic."

Trev sounded like he was trying to make me feel better, and I snuck a glance at him to find him grinning from ear to ear.

"You don't seem upset about this turn of events."

"We just got out of a ten year prison sentence. What's to be upset about?"

"Nothing, but… were we seriously in danger of going to prison, just for showing up here with some asshats following us?"

It was Rhelia who answered, and I couldn't help but notice that she seemed unable to repress a smile of her own.

"For leading MOME officers through a hidden seam into Unterberg, the council would gladly have killed you, if they thought you'd done it on purpose. As it is, a ten year sentence was relatively light, considering how many MOME agents are still unaccounted for on the streets here now. Plus, your sentence would have had the bonus of luring the MOME agents to Regnadevarg, the most defensible hold in the entire city. The council will be… disappointed that they were forced to let you go. I imagine they will be contacting my Matriarch immediately to ensure that I am not lying."

"I'm not sure that explanation made any sense to me, but if they thought you were lying, why wouldn't they just confront you about it right there, while they still had us?"

Rhelia's smile only grew.

"It will take very careful wording to confirm the truth with my Matriarch without starting a diplomatic incident, as it is. They could never have confronted me openly without risking war with the dragons."

"I have definitely missed a few key details," I mumbled.

"Worry not, Living Cat. You are a dragon sssssissssster now, you will learn all that you need to learn in good time."

I looked hopelessly between Rhelia and Trev.

"Well, at least this answers my question about whether or not Rhelia was the girlfriend you were talking about," I said.

That only made Rhelia and Trev laugh so loudly that the walls almost shook, as we descended an ornately decorated staircase that covered the distance from whatever they called the drizzle palace that housed the council into an open square full of people, pigeons, and…

"Fuck. MOME agents," Trev muttered, just before bursting into flames.

O F COURSE, WHEN Trev bursts into flames it's not as disconcerting as it would be if someone else were to do it. After all, when someone spends half of their time as a flaming bird anyway, random combustion is par for the course. But that didn't mean I was used to it. Still, surprising as it might have been, it was nothing compared to seeing Rhelia become a dragon large enough to fill the entire square.

I tried to shout "holy fuck!" but the words were swallowed as I was dragged involuntarily into my snow leopard form. I didn't waste time being pissed about it, because I was too busy trying to figure out where the dragon ended and the bad guys began, so I could whoop a little bit of MOME ass. As it happened though, Trev and I were surrounded by ebon scales that shone with the same silvery irides-cence that coated Rhelia's skin, and I couldn't find a single gap between us and the bad guys.

Of course, Trev, in his fiery, winged form, wasn't hampered by the circle of serpent that enclosed us. He just shot into the sky straight above us and started circling.

Do not engage, little onessss, Rhelia's voice spoke directly into my (and I assumed Trevor's) mind, even as I was trying to gain purchase on her scales in order to launch myself over the heap of dragon tail that lay between me and the MOME agents.

What's up with the overprotective act? I asked Trev, who was now diving for a patch of cobbled square next to me, as a streak of some nasty-looking spell flew through the air he'd occupied only a moment earlier.

There are some rules of dragonkind that make it very tricky for us to fight MOME now that Rhelia has declared us kin, Trev replied, as he landed beside me.

So why'd you shift to phoenix and start calling attention to yourself? I asked, genuinely curious.

Well, now that they've very clearly shot at me, in full view of witnesses, Rhelia can claim she was defending her kin if it ever comes up. They violated the treaty first, so her Matriarch will be forced to acknowledge that she was provoked.

I decided that dragon politics were complicated and that I'd ask more questions later, then tried to focus on what was going on in the square outside of our little circle of serpent. Unfortunately, I couldn't see shit, and all I could hear was what sounded like a jet engine roaring to life periodically, and a few truly agonized screams.

A few moments later the smell of barbecue filled the square, and I tried not to retch as my brain attached the meaning of burning meat smell to the sudden quiet that now surrounded us, and its significance.

"Umm… I think I might throw up," I muttered, not even noticing that I'd returned to human form, along with Trev and Rhelia beside me. I closed my eyes before I could take in the heinous scene that I was sure was waiting for me, and swallowed hard.

"You are so weak of constitution, Living Cat? Do you think the agents of MOME would have spared you from an equally gruesome fate?"

I expected the next breath I took to be laced with an even more disconcerting smell of charred meat, but when it instead came with the smell of crisp, clean air, I decided to risk opening my eyes. There was a giant scorch mark before us, but there was no trace of flesh left, only a few tiny wisps of ash that were already blowing away on the wind.

"Well, that was cleaner than I expected," I said, as the churning that my stomach had been doing earlier was replaced with a leaden feeling instead. The MOME agents were still deader than dead, and I wasn't entirely sure how I felt about that, even though Rhelia was probably right about the fate they had planned for me, but at least I wasn't staring at barbecued human. I supposed the one whiff I'd caught of charring flesh was just what the wind had still carried from the instant in which the deed had been done.

Rhelia stared at me for a moment, as though she were trying to decide whether or not she should be insulted, so I tried to compose my features.

"Look," I said. "I don't think you're monstrous for destroying the people who were attacking someone you love. I just… I'm not used to killing people, and I was expecting to see charred human remains everywhere, so… forgive me if it takes me some time to adjust. And… I can't promise I'll ever be ok with the whole killing people thing, even if they deserve it. It's just… really final."

To my shock, Rhelia smiled, wrapping me in an embrace.

"You will make an exsssscellent dragon," she said, delivering a quick kiss on my cheek before letting me go.

Since I had no idea what *that* meant, I decided to change the subject.

"So, how do we find everyone else?"

Rhelia smiled. "Follow me."

I'M NOT SURE what I'd expected when Rhelia had told us to follow her, then strode purposefully through the large cobbled square that she'd just left half-scorched and drifting in the ash of immolated MOME agents, but her leading us to a meticulously maintained, topiary filled garden that took up as much space as the palace behind us, walking into the center of what appeared to be a solid tree larger than even the biggest sequoia I'd ever seen photos of, and disappearing save for a single ebon-skinned hand that reached out and beckoned us to follow, was not it.

I didn't even have time to take in the details of the green space that surrounded us before Trev pushed me forward and I was stumbling, reaching for Rhelia's hand out of a desperate wish not to fall, more than anything else. Her slender fingers caught mine with a strength that seemed far beyond their scope, supporting me without even dipping under my sudden weight. Trev followed close behind, with a hand still on my shoulder, and I wondered if we were really standing in the middle of a tree, or if we were just in some dark space that could have been anywhere. The faint glow from Rhelia's skin was the only light in the space, but it did nothing to illuminate whatever surrounded us, only made her faintly visible in the darkness and made me able to see my own hand in hers.

Before I could ask where we were, or what we were doing, Rhelia made a strange hissing sound that resembled no language that I had ever heard before, then moved her hands as if she were parting an invisible curtain.

Only, suddenly, the curtain wasn't invisible, it was a giant, shimmering, shuddering thing, like aurora borealis in a tangible form, and she was parting it, and Trev was pushing me while Rhelia pulled me with her other hand and… then it was all gone, and we were standing in the middle of a green meadow dotted with wildflowers, surrounded by snowcapped peaks.

"Where in the seven hells—" I was cut off by a great shadow eclipsing the sun, as a dragon's head filled my vision so completely that I thought the entire sky had been swallowed.

"Child, what in the realms have you done?" The dragon's head—presumably attached to a body, but I couldn't see that far—asked, blinking a reptilian eye so large it could easily have been the moon.

"I thought we were agreed that I wassss no longer a child, Vereneth," Rhelia said, from where she stood next to me.

"I thought so as well, but you have brought strangers into this realm twice today, and I can sense that these two carry something more ominous with them than the mere status of refugees." The dragon sniffed as it spoke.

Its giant slitted nostrils, curving at the top of its enormous snout, flared and smoked, as a second set of eyelids—perpendicular to the first set I'd noticed—opened and closed twice. I tried to take in more details of the giant creature, since I hadn't been able to see most of Rhelia properly the one time that she shown her dragon form in front of me, but I could barely process what I was seeing, I was so awed by its massive eye and cavernous mouth, which contained a deadly array of teeth so large they might as well have been marble columns. It had horns that rose from its head, twisting and curving like the most enormous junipers I'd ever seen. They were similarly silvered, and, indeed, the dragon itself was a deep bronze color, like a mix of aged wood and burnished metal.

"Thesssse two aren't refugeessss, they are dragon kin," Rhelia replied, her chin held high in defiance.

The giant serpent before us turned away and released a gout of flame so hot, I felt my eyebrows singe away, even from a distance of a hundred feet from where it had released its ire.

"That will take some explaining," it said tersely, when it turned back to us. I wondered briefly if I'd soiled myself. I'd certainly felt scared enough, but I must have been dehydrated and underfed, because my pants appeared to be dry.

"Then let ussss meet with the elderssss sssso I do not need to repeat myssssself," Rhelia replied.

~~~

If Vereneth had made me want to wet myself, the circle of elders made me wish I'd never been born. I didn't know if the dragons had some enchantment on them that induced fear in all who viewed them, or if it was just my body's natural reaction to being confronted with a predator that so clearly outmatched me, but I found it difficult to look any
~~~

of them in the eye, or even stare directly at them for long. The only thing that allowed me to see more than an eyeball of any of the behemoths was my vantage point atop a giant column, or maybe it was a tiny but very tall plateau, it was difficult to say. At any rate, I was at least a hundred feet up on a natural platform, along with Trev and Rhelia, and we were surrounded by about thirty dragons, each the size of a cruise liner, a few of them larger than shipping freighters. I had asked where Sol, Seamus, Albert and the refugees were, as we'd made our way to… whatever this column thing was, but I'd only gotten a few vague assurances that they were nearby and safe before I'd been distracted by the most terrifying sight of my life.

I hated myself for the fear that coursed through my body, because I had always considered myself a dragon person. I mean… every time I read a fantasy book, I hoped there would be dragons in it. And if there were dragons, I wanted them to be good guys, or at least neutral. I hated the stories in which dragons were unthinking menaces. If a fantasy author wanted my money, then dragons needed to at least be thoughtful and compelling villains. Books in which humans and dragons worked together were my favorite, although I wasn't overly fond of the ones where humans treated dragons like horses. I'd never been particularly keen on the idea of dragons being tame and loyal beasts. It seemed unlikely that an apex predator could ever find humans useful enough for that to be a good deal.

So, the fact that I was nearly pissing myself just looking at these creatures made me feel like the worlds biggest fraud. After a childhood of imagining how cool it would be to meet a real dragon, back when I was still convinced they existed, my response now made my cheeks warm with humiliation. I mean sure, they were giant and imposing creatures that could kill me with a single bite, or perhaps even an accidental sneeze, but they were clearly beings who could be reasoned with. So there was no need for me to be standing atop a tower of rock shaking like a reed in a strong wind.

"You can sssstop your glamorssss," Rhelia, still in human form, called out from her perch beside me.

My head snapped to attention. The thirty behemoths that formed a giant circle around us all grumbled.

"You would dare to frighten my family ssssoooo, without causssse?" Rhelia asked. The grumbling cut off abruptly, replaced by a silence that sounded like it might break with bloodshed.

"Your family?" a thunderous voice from directly across the circle boomed. It came from a dragon covered from snout to tail in glinting silver scales.

Rhelia inclined her head deferentially for a moment before replying.

"Trevor Marmot issss my mate, and hissss ssssis-ssster issss therefore my sssssisssster."

The uproar that followed that announcement made me long for the silence that had greeted her last statement, but I noticed that the fear that had encompassed me earlier had fled. I was able to stand at my full height and look every one of those giants in the eye.

"Were they enchanting me to fear them?" I asked Trev, over my shoulder.

"Not just you, I was about to poop my pants," Trev admitted, in a stage whisper.

I would have laughed, but Rhelia looked like she was about to go hulk on someone's ass, and I didn't want to miss the show.

"You dare quesssstion my choicsssse of mate?" She didn't shout, but her voice thundered from where we stood atop the raised bit of earth that held us, and I wondered if she was magnifying it magically, or if it was simply the acoustics of where we stood. Regardless, all thirty of the voices that had been grumbling in unison now quieted.

"Rhelia, you are young to make such a choice at all, and… a human? Do you wish to spend so much of your existence alone?"

That was a different dragon, one covered in scales of jade, but almost as large as the silver behemoth that had spoken earlier.

"Not a mere human, a phoenixssss. And if I am old enough to rissssk my life for our realm, then I am old enough to choosssse whom to sssspend that life with."

"So… you guys are more than just dating, huh?" I asked Trev, out of the corner of my mouth. Communicating telepathically seemed like a terrible idea, since Rhelia could always hear me and I had no idea whether her fellow dragons shared that ability or not. They might easily hear us where we were, but I was tired of not knowing what was going on, and if thirty dragons were about to decide to kill me, I wanted to know why.

Trev chuckled, but it was Rhelia who replied.

"Sssssissssster, I will exssssplain all of the dragon cusssstomssss that you musssst know sssssoon enough, but know that dragonssss mate for life, and we live a *very* long time."

"Yikes," I muttered. "No shopping around first?"

Rhelia smiled, turning to face me fully. I was once again entranced by the way her ebon skin and iridescent sheen caught the light of the sun.

"We are allowed to 'shop around,' assss you ssssay, and often we live our whole livessss without choossssssing a mate, but when we find ssssomeone worthy, we treasssssure it beyond all thingssss."

"Sounds stifling," I quipped.

"No one ssssssaid we cannot have loverssss," she replied, smirking before turning back to the elders that encircled us.

I stared at Trev for a moment, but he just shook his head at me and wrapped his fingers in Rhelia's.

Ok. Score one for the dragons. Boy, did I have a million questions about how their society worked. In particular, why it was such a big deal to pick a mate if you could still be polyamorous?

It's mostly about having kids, Trev sent to me.

Well, that just launched a thousand other questions.

"You have served us well, Rhelia, and we appreciate all that you have done for this realm, which is why we would hate to see you squander yourself with a human who can do so little to serve your family," said the silver dragon.

"You act assss though the deed issss not already done," Rhelia said.

I was about to snickeringly ask if "the deed" was what I thought it was (because, yeah, sometimes I have the sense of humor of a twelve-year-old), but then Rhelia slid into her enormous serpentine self, and Trev went with her, transforming into his phoenix form. Both of them launched skyward, leaving me behind on the earthen pedestal as they careened through the sky, dancing together in an intricate pattern that brought tears to my eyes. Trev seemed somehow magnified by the dance, and his phoenix form loomed larger than I had ever seen it, until he appeared to almost match the size of Rhelia in all her ebon-scaled, iridescent glory. They twined round each other, weaving in and out of patterns that looked as though they'd been rehearsed for hundreds of years. If I hadn't known that Trev was exactly as old as I was (give or take a few minutes), I would have thought them ancient partners.

Apparently, I wasn't the only one. When they landed, the surrounding dragons made a low, resonant sound that felt like it was going to reduce the pillar we stood on to dust. Since Rhelia and Trev returned to their human forms and bowed, I took that sound to signify approval.

"Come," Rhelia said, nodding at Trev and me. "Let them prepare the fessssstivitiesssss. There isssss much to exssssssplain."

I nodded and followed, wondering how much stranger my life could possibly get.

~~~

The answer was a fair bit.

Rhelia spent the next few hours explaining to me the various intricacies of dragon culture, most of which, I won't lie, I didn't fully understand. There was a crazy hierarchy that sounded like it would take years to fully comprehend, and all the cultural subtleties seemed to stem from that hierarchy. The key points were mainly that Rhelia had saved our asses in Unterberg by declaring Trev her mate, because it meant that the Unterberg rulers couldn't touch us thanks to a treaty struck up long ago between the dragons and Unterberg. They couldn't touch us because Trev being Rhelia's mate made us dragonkin.

I thought that title was purely superficial when Rhelia first explained it. Like, we were in-laws and it would be a political disaster to mess with us. Rhelia hinted that there was more to it than that, but
~~~

she said that she couldn't explain what until after the ceremony.

"What ceremony?"

"Your induction," she said.

"*My* induction? What do I have to do with any of this?"

"You are my ssssisssster now. And, assss you are not of age by dragon sssstandardssss and you have no parentssss, you will need a guardian. Luckily, an older ssssissssster issss allowed to be a guardian if she issss of her majority."

"Umm… what do you mean, I'm not of age? How old do I have to be, to not be under your guardianship? And what the hells does that even mean?"

"You musssst be one hundred yearssss old to reach your majority in the dragon realmssss."

"Seriously? Wait. How old are you?"

"One hundred and sssseven," she replied, placidly.

"Does Trev know?" I asked, before I could stop myself. She laughed.

"Yesss. He issss not concerned. If I were a human, I would only be a teenager, that issss why my human form lookssss the way it doessss. Dragonssss live a *very* long time."

I nodded and shut my mouth. I mean hey, if Trev knew and was cool with it, then… well, Rhelia seemed like a badass to me. It's not like she was anyone's grandmother.

"So do dragons live to be a thousand, then?" I asked, doing some math and rounding up.

Rhelia laughed.

"No, dragonssss lowered the age of majority after the influxssss of dragon shifterssss during the purgessss on earth. The age of majority ussssed to be five hundred, but with dragon shifterssss not living quite assss long assss full dragonssss, the age was moved to 100."

"So dragon shifters live to be a thousand?"

"Ssssometimessss two thoussssand, it variessss."

"And full dragons?"

She shrugged.

"The oldesssst are… *very* old."

I made myself close my mouth.

"Right, ok. So, were they right about you dooming yourself to a life of loneliness after Trev dies?"

She sighed and shook her head.

"For reassssonssss that are too numeroussss to lisssst at the moment, we think it likely that Trev might outlive *me*, but regardlessss of that, I wouldn't have chossssen differently. He *issss* my mate."

"You make it sound like it's just a part of who he is, like it's not a choice."

Rhelia sighed and started unbuttoning the silky shirt she was wearing. I considered objecting, but for one thing, I'd already learned that shifters were way less restrained about nudity than most people, and for another, I doubted that Rhelia was just stripping in front of me for funzies.

When she got halfway down her shirt, she pulled the collar open and exposed her chest from the sternum up. Spread across it was the most beautiful tattoo I'd ever seen. In a bright, sparkling white that contrasted starkly with the ebon shade of her skin, the outline of a phoenix in full flame glowed like starlight. It was so entrancing that I began to think it was moving.

"Isn't it considered bad form to get a tattoo of your significant other?" I asked, despite how awed I was by the beauty of the mark.

To my surprise, she laughed.

"It issss not a tattoo. I have carried thissss mark ssssince birth."

"Umm… that's one hell of a birthmark."

"A sssseeer attendssss the birth or hatching of every dragonling, ssssometimessss they name a child, ssssometimessss they lay a mark upon them, ssssometimessss they do nothing at all. Thissss issss the mark I wassss given momentssss after I wassss born."

I sighed, not knowing what I was supposed to say, or even believe, for that matter. That Rhelia and my brother were somehow fated for each other? I'd never bought into that concept. I even struggled to swallow the idea when it was wrapped up in a fairy tale or fantasy novel.

"It's beautiful," I said, because that much was true.

"You do not believe in fate?" Rhelia asked, after a long and awkward pause.

I shook my head.

"Good," she said, stunning me enough to make me meet her eyes again. "Neither do I. I do not think that thissss mark meanssss that I *have* to love your brother, or that we have no choicsssse but to be together… but when I met him, it felt like a missssing part of my ssssoul returned to me, and I only later learned that he wassss a phoenixssss."

I could read the embarrassment in Rhelia's face, like all this talk of love made her feel childish. So, I decided to woman up.

"Rhelia, if you love my brother and want to be with him forever, you don't have to justify it to me. And whether it's fate, or just a weird cosmic coincidence, or even just a really solid gimmick to get my brother to join some weird cult, you have my blessing."

I paused for a second, and Rhelia just stared at me.

"Ok. Fine, you don't have my blessing if this is just a ploy to get him to join some weird cult."

She finally laughed.

"I'm all for Trev loving a dragon." I continued. "I mean, so far you seem like a badass and, more importantly, from what I can tell, you're a good person. You saved a whole bunch of children and found a place for them here in your secret realm that no one is ever allowed to enter, *and* you love my twin brother, which shows that you have excellent taste in humans."

When she still didn't say anything I added, "Look, it's not like you two need my approval or anything, but for what it's worth, you have it. Now tell me what the hell it means that I have to be your ward until I'm a hundred."

And so she did.

The short version? After a ceremony in which I would swear loyalty to the dragon realm before all others, I would become official dragonkin, and after that I would get to find out all kinds of cool things about the dragons. Then Rhelia would be responsible for me, and if I fucked up at all it would be her fault, as far as all the dragons were concerned. I didn't like the idea of shucking responsibility that way, but she said we didn't have much choice in the matter, and she trusted me not to do anything that might get her banished or killed. Then she gave me a rundown on the things that might do that. The biggest ones were revealing the secrets of how to enter the dragon realm to an outsider, or somehow contributing to the death of a dragon. After that, I was given a basic breakdown on dragon history. It was long and boring and by the end of it my brain hurt. The highlights? MOME treated the dragons just as poorly as they treated everyone else, if not worse. Luckily, dragons have always been good seekers (which I learned was the name for folks who could sense seams— seams, of course, being the interdimensional pockets that let someone get from say, a back alley in La Paz to a hidden kingdom the size of Manhattan or, say, a realm filled entirely with big-assed mountains, fresh air, dragons, and dragonkin).

Before I really felt like I had a solid understanding of... well, anything (and wasn't that just par for the course these days?), I was being ushered out of Rhelia's cave-like, though well furnished, dwelling, and led to the ceremony.

THE VIEW FROM the top of the pillar this time was both less and more intimidating. It was less intimidating in that it looked kind of like a party. That is, if a party consisted of a thousand dragons of all shapes, sizes, and colors, scrambling all around the elder circles making as much noise as a hundred freight trains, and doing everything from slumbering peacefully to flitting about the sky like overexcited bats. Many were decorated with bright jewels and feathers.

I was still wearing jeans and a T-shirt, but had been crammed into an ornate feathered headdress that I was convinced was a rather elaborate prank that Rhelia was pulling on me, which she would spend the next hundred years laughing about.

If I lived that long.

Ok. I was probably overreacting. No one had said anything about the dragonkin ceremony being potentially dangerous. I didn't *think* that the elders would eat me if I messed up somehow, but Rhelia had cautioned me to "Be ssssure that you mean the wordssss of the oath when you ssssay them." In addition to that, I was told, just before Rhelia flew me up to the top of the pillar, that there would be a test of some kind.

"Do not worry, Living Cat," she had reassured me. "I am ssssure that you will do very well."

That was scant reassurance when it was the first I'd heard of any kind of test and it was approximately ninety seconds before said test was scheduled to happen.

I thought over the words in the oath that Rhelia had helped me memorize, not an hour earlier, and thought about whether or not I meant them. I thought I did, but honestly, I'd only been introduced to the dragon realm a few hours ago. What if the whole lot turned out to be a band of deranged miscreants who only sought power over the other realms, or wanted to sacrifice virgins at every full moon, or some such shit? I mean, nothing I'd seen so far made me think that was likely, but whatever, I hadn't pegged Edik as a vampire stalker the first time I'd met him either. Evil lurked behind surprising corners.

I supposed I would just have to trust that Trev's judgment in partners was sound, and that the culture that had created my brother's life mate was a good one.

Fingers crossed.

"Victoria Marmot," boomed one of the thunderous voices that had addressed Rhelia earlier, when she had been declaring her mating to Trev, "are you prepared to pledge your loyalty to the Realm of Dragons?"

"I am," I replied, hoping desperately that I would remember all the words to the oath, and not fuck it up.

"Then you may begin," the voice called, across the now hushing crowd of dragons below me.

"In solemn bond with the blood of wings and serpents, I profess my loyalty to the Realm of Fang and Claw. I swear never to betray its people or its place. I swear to protect my people and my home with everything that I am."

As I said the words, I felt the air around me warm, and a buzz, like the hum just before lightning strikes, enveloped me. I was getting ready to leap from my perch, sure that a freak weather event was about to wipe me out, when the hum ceased abruptly and I was plunged instantly into darkness.

"What the fuck? Why can't I see?" I muttered into the void. I could still feel earth beneath my feet, but I could no longer hear the sounds of the dragon crowd that had filled the circle below me, nor could I see anything, not even my own hand when I raised it up to wave in front of my face.

"Hello? No one told me that going blind was going to be part of the ceremony."

I heard nothing save my own voice, but I… felt?… laughter.

"Who's there?" I asked, hoping I wasn't about to join the ranks of people who say those words just prior to dying horribly.

No one is here, Living Cat, said a voice in the darkness, which I could tell wasn't Rhelia's even though it had used her nickname for me.

"Great. Am I going to be stuck with that name forever because of Rhelia's crap sense of humor?" I asked.

I do not think it is such a 'crap' name, as you call it. It is both amusing and accurate. You should treasure it. Good names are difficult to come by. Besides, the name you use is not your true name, and we need a true name to call you by.

I snorted, not impressed, but I supposed it could have been worse.

"At least it's accurate and not insulting."

Indeed, replied the voice in my head, "sounding" amused. I suppose it was more that I felt its amusement, as though it shed some of its emotion to me, but it certainly didn't "sound" amused, since it didn't sound at all.

"May I ask who I'm speaking to?"

You may ask. Does the answer matter? Do you know who any of us are by name?

"Fair point. How about sending along an image of what you look like? My guess would be that I saw you earlier today at the elder's council."

Smart cat, the voice replied. And then my mind was filled with the image of a behemoth of a dragon, not quite as large as the gold and silver dragon that had questioned Rhelia, but only slightly smaller, and with scales of a brilliant indigo hue.

"You have beautiful scales," I said, without thinking, then hastily added, "I don't know if your culture values physical beauty or not, or what a dragon would find beautiful if it does, but... I really like that shade of blue."

Thank you, child. I am pleased that my colors please you.

I took a deep breath and let it out. It occurred to me in that moment that it had been a bit insane to agree to go through this ceremony in a culture that

I knew almost nothing about. Oh well. It was a bit late for cold feet at this point.

"Is this the test?" I asked, when only silence followed the dragon's last statement.

Mmm… it might be. What do you think?

"If it is, I have no idea what I'm being tested on, but then again, since I was only made aware that there even was a test a few seconds before I came up here, that's not saying much."

Tell me, Living Cat, what you see in the darkness.

I refrained from saying that it was a stupid question. I also refrained from making a comment about dramatics, fantasy novels, and plot twists that were driven by surprise tests and challenges. Gwen wasn't here, and she was my narrator, the one I expected to appreciate literary criticisms of my own story. So I swallowed my glib remarks. I saw nothing in the darkness. That was the thing about darkness, wasn't it? It doesn't show you much.

But then, slowly, as though someone were approaching with candle from over a mile away on a moonless night, something began to take shape.

It took me a very long moment to figure out what I was seeing, but when I did, it filled me with the warm fuzzies, almost literally. As though arriving from far away, I began to make out the shape of a snow leopard coming into focus. It was difficult to tell from this distance, especially considering how few times I had actually seen it, but something about it felt instinctually familiar.

"That's my snow leopard form," I said, before I even had time to question the notion myself.

Indeed? Excellent. Now if you'll just—

But the voice was cut off by my gasp, as something much larger approached behind the furry figure, a form that I felt such a deep familiarity with, even though I'd only had a week or so to get to know it.

What is it, child? What do you see?

If I had known what the test was supposed to be about, or how anything in this new world I'd been dumped into was supposed to work, I might have kept my next words to myself, but as it was, I was too awed, and far too unsuspecting, to hold my tongue.

"I... it's... I think it's a dragon. I mean, it's a small one, judging by all the ones I've seen today, but... it's got wings, a long slender body like a snake's, a head... a head kind of like a horse's but with giant horns, covered in scales, and it's... it's all silver. It looks as if it should be embroidered onto a kimono."

The voice was silent for a long time.

Do you see anything else? it eventually asked.

I waited, but nothing else appeared behind the dragon, which swirled peacefully in the darkness above and behind the more familiar snow leopard. I had never seen the dragon before, but something about it felt incredibly comfortable—known, the same way the snow leopard felt to me even though I'd only ever *seen* it once in the mirror and otherwise had been too busy dodging people trying to kill me to get a good look at the form itself. Besides that, there was nothing in the darkness, save a tiny ball of light far in the distance.

How intriguing, the voice said, after I explained that I only saw those two forms and the ball of light. *Let us return.*

And with that, I was surrounded once more by light and sound, and saw the crowd of dragons waiting with quiet anticipation as I blinked away the darkness.

The same voice that had sounded in my head now sounded out loud to the entire crowd.

"The Living Cat has looked into the darkness and seen the light, she has said her oath true, and she has been granted the finding of seams. She will forever be called dragonkin and shall enjoy a true drago—"

I didn't hear what followed, because at that moment a familiar hand grabbed my wrist.

"Seriously, Gwen?" I said, glaring at her. "Now is not a good time."

"Seamus and Sol need you," she said, before she pulled me through time and space.

I HAD *THOUGHT* that Seamus and Sol were safely tucked away in the dragon realm. That's where I'd expected to find them when I'd asked where they were and Rhelia had replied that we should follow her. And then the first dragon that had confronted us had straight up talked about the refugees that Rhelia had brought through earlier. I had assumed Sol and Seamus were busy settling the kids in or something, but I had figured once I was officially dragonkin, whatever that meant, I would be able to see them.

So having Gwen show up saying they needed me and then blinking us out of existence was more than a little disturbing.

Which meant that for the first time in my entire life, I was relieved to see Edik.

Even though he was attacking Sol and Seamus, who had their backs up against Sol's cottage, and was screaming something incoherent while he repeatedly tried to bite them.

I sighed.

Then I shifted directly behind him and put him in a headlock.

"Edik, I give zero fucks about what you are doing here, but you have precisely 30 seconds to make me care enough not to rip your throat from your neck."

When he sagged in my arms, I relaxed my grip just enough to let him speak.

"My darling Victoria, I—"

I cut him off by tightening the hold once again.

"Let me make this part really clear. I'm not your darling anything, and any references to me as such will lose you ten seconds of time to explain. Try again. Twenty seconds. Go."

"These heathens won't tell me where my daughter is! They have hidden her from me, and I can no longer sense her. Where is she!? She is so frail, she needs me, she cannot make her way in this world withou—"

I cut him off again.

"Is she with the others?" I asked Sol and Seamus, who both looked as exhausted as I felt. No wonder, they'd been struggling against raging vampire. They nodded.

"Great. Then she's safe. Edik, your daughter is safe and that's all I can tell you. I've been sworn to secrecy regarding her location, but you're just going to have to trust me. Or I can just kill you. I'm really fine either way, at this point."

That wasn't strictly true. I loathed Edik pretty substantially at this point, but I still didn't know if I'd be able to kill him. Not if he didn't attack me first, at least. I didn't think I had it in me to snap his neck right now, for example, if all he did was beg me to let him see his daughter. Then again, if it had looked like he was really going to hurt Sol or Seamus, he'd probably be dead already. Regardless, I certainly didn't have the time or energy to coach Edik through knowing where his daughter was. If she was still with the other children rescued from MOME, I had to assume that was where she wanted to be. I couldn't imagine Seamus or Sol trying to keep her with the group against her will, and if a teenaged girl wanted to get away from her parents so badly that she was willing to stay in the dragon realm with a group of total strangers, I was not going to get in her way.

I dropped Edik to the ground, stepped forward to grab Seamus and Sol by the wrists, and shifted us all inside Sol's cabin.

Where I almost fell to the floor from the intense heat that rolled through my abdomen, making my toes curl.

Holy fuck, I felt like I was going to burst and the only thing that would stop me was getting in bed with Sol and Seamus right now.

I dropped their wrists like they were on fire and ran to lock the door, hoping neither of them could tell how turned on I was. My whole body felt flushed, and I wondered how it was even possible to be this attracted to two people at the same time. I took a few deep breaths and tried to tell myself that it was just relief at seeing them safe and alive.

When I looked up, they both looked like deer about to be taken down by a Mack truck. What was wrong with us?

"I'm really glad to see you guys," I said, desperate to distract myself from the molten longing that consumed me. "I thought you were back in the dragon realm, though."

Sol swallowed, licked her lips, and then swallowed again. I tried not to watch every move like it set my skin alight, but I failed.

"We were. Rhelia took us there with the kids from MOME, but her matriarch decided that we were no longer needed and offered to send us home. We had no idea where you were, so…"

She trailed off and I couldn't help but notice that she seemed to be watching the rise and fall of my chest. For some reason that made my nipples harden, and I had to swallow a moan. What the fuck? Five minutes ago I had been in the middle of some weird assed dragon rite of passage, three minutes ago I'd had my vampire stalker in a head-lock. I had so many more important things to think about than whether or not Sol was staring at my chest. What was wrong with me?

"When we got here, that asshat was waiting for us, screaming his head off about his precious Renata, and then when we refused to tell him where she was, he started trying to bite us. As if his damned vampire venom would even work on a strong were." She sighed, and my own eyes were drawn to the rise and fall of *her* chest in a way that was completely inappropriate to the conversation.

"We'd already fought off five MOME agents today…. It's a good thing you got here when you did," Seamus said, but his voice sounded rough.

Before I could even take a good look at Seamus, or ask what was going on, he rushed to the door, muttered, "I'll be back in a minute, just going for a run," and slipped out so fast I wondered if I'd even locked it.

I should have been worried about Seamus running into Edik, or getting cold, or getting lost, or something, but instead all I could think about was how I wanted him back here so I could have my way with him. Ugh… what was wrong with my brain? Seriously, even teenage hormones didn't explain this kind of single-minded lust.

I almost voiced the question, but then Sol stepped up to me and I could feel the heat rolling off of her body in waves. I hadn't ever been with a woman before, but I now knew deep in my bones that I wanted to be with Sol. I wanted to run my tongue over every curve of her body, and explore… everywhere.

She leaned against me, and suddenly I couldn't think of anything else at all.

"Gatita, I know we haven't known each other very long, but do you…" her voice trailed off, hestitant.

"Want to take you into that bedroom and learn everything I can about how to pleasure a woman?" I finished for her. "Yes. Yes, I do.

ROM THERE A few sizzling kisses quickly progressed to an incredibly hot sex scene that I'm not going to relate to you, because that's not the point of this story. I will say, however, that I was surprised by how good it was, considering that first time sexual encounters with a new partner aren't always very good and also that it was my first time with a woman at all. I had expected more awkwardness. Instead, we both finished at the same time with a pair of mind-blowing orgasms. I didn't think it was that suspicious at the time, but afterwards…

Well, anyway, I had been on the cusp of initiating round two when a familiar voice announced, "I'm afraid the two of you are needed elsewhere."

I nearly jumped off the bed as that voice doused me like a cold a shower.

"Ack! Fuck, Gwen! You can't just show up like that when people are getting it on!"

She was standing just inside the door like it was no big deal.

"You'd be surprised how often I show up like that when people are getting it on, actually."

"What?!"

"Goddess of fortune, remember? For some folks that's all about makin' babies."

"Ugh… Gwen, why are you here?" I asked. Sol had been surprisingly quiet, but unlike me (trying to cover myself with whatever bit of blanket I could grab) she was just lying there casually, as though she spent most of her time naked on a bed, with another woman, expecting random deities to show up and announce things. And hell, for all I knew, maybe she did.

"Seamus needs you," Gwen said, then poofed out of existence.

Luckily, she only poofed as far as the living room. I could hear her rustling around the small kitchen, likely looking for tea paraphernalia. I guess she was giving us some privacy to wrap things up. Sol kissed me in a soft lingering manner that promised all kinds of fun was to be had later, then grabbed her clothes and walked out of the room. I chuckled at the thought of her not giving two fucks about strutting around naked and then put on my own jeans, shoved the ladies back into my sports bra, and pulled on a hoodie. Then I did my best to think of things other than the amazing sex we'd just had, but largely failed.

I took a deep breath and walked out into the kitchen.

Gwen was busily fussing with a teapot and Sol had put on pants and a bra, an outfit I didn't object to in the least, but found incredibly distracting. I couldn't get the feel and taste of her out of my mind, and every time I looked at her, I instantly started replaying everything we'd just done to one another.

That was weird. I didn't usually find sex to be all-consuming. I had thought the way we felt before Seamus had run out was just an anomaly.

I walked over to stand beside Sol, and almost purred when she put her hand on my back and started sliding it under my hoodie. My skin caught fire wherever she ran her fingers, and all I could think of was dragging her back to bed.

Focus power, Vic. Come on.

I mentally shook myself, trying to pay attention to Gwen and her tea.

Sol's hand wandered up the front of my hoodie and began sliding over my sports bra, making me thoroughly ready to pull her back into the bedroom to have my way with her again, when Gwen must have dropped the teapot. A loud shattering noise briefly took my attention away from Sol.

"Damn it," Gwen said, looking between us. "It's happening already."

"What is?" I asked, leaning into the feel of Sol's hand playing over both of my breasts. I ducked my head and kissed her shoulder.

"That damned mating bond!" Gwen said, clapping her hands, presumably to get our attention, but I was too busy kissing my way towards Sol's exposed cleavage to care.

"Mating bond?" Sol asked, sounding vaguely concerned. "Can't be, we're not a mating pair. No testes."

Her hand had never stopped roaming my breasts, and now she was pinching gently at my nipples through my sports bra. Apparently neither of us were at all concerned that Gwen was standing right there, cleaning up fragments of shattered teapot.

I had started running my fingers under the fabric of her bra, and she was leaning her head back in exaltation.

"Well, then how do you explain your sudden inability to keep your hands off each other?" Gwen asked.

Sol snorted.

"Because we just had some of the best sex of my life," she muttered, grabbing my breasts more forcefully and bringing her other hand under my hoodie to join the fun.

"And mine," I seconded, running my tongue along the tops of her breasts again.

"And how common is that between two people who've never had sex with each other before?" Gwen asked.

I shrugged, knowing that Gwen had a point, but not really caring. Sol sat up a bit though, and her hands paused in their task, which made me growl a bit.

"And how often does a woman who has never been with another woman before know every move that will push her partner right over the edge?" Gwen continued.

Sol stopped everything and dropped her hands, and then I really did growl.

"We can't have a mating bond," Sol objected. "Those are for pairs that can procreate. My kind never have them."

Gwen just looked between us. Sol looked at me and stepped back.

"What. The. Fuck. Is. A. Mating. Bond?" I gritted out.

"It's an unbreakable lifelong bond between two weres," Sol replied.

"Two or more," Gwen corrected.

"Multi-way mating bonds are a myth," Sol replied.

Gwen shrugged.

"Suit yourself."

"What are you two talking about?" I asked, through the haze of lust that was clouding my mind. Now that I considered it, thinking was a lot harder than it should have been. All my body seemed to want to do was pin Sol down to the bed in the other room with various forms of pleasure. As I forced myself to think through the fog of lust, I had to recognize that even though she was hot, and we'd just had amazing sex, something was definitely not right about the single-mindedness of this.

"What is going on?" I asked, finally snapping out of things enough to understand how strange this was. I tried to take a step back from Sol, but found it was a surprisingly difficult proposition. My body did not want to move away from hers, no matter what my brain told it.

"Gwen is suggesting that we've somehow become a mated pair," Sol said, still sounding incredulous. "But that's not possible, because that doesn't happen to same-sex couples."

"It does sometimes," Gwen corrected.

"Only in legends," Sol scoffed. "Not in the real world."

Gwen only shrugged again.

"Why would the mating bond snap into place for two women? We can't MATE, not in the sense that Gaia, or whoever decides these things, would approve of, anyway."

"Maybe the gods have gotten more progressive," Gwen suggested.

I laughed.

"You would know if they had, wouldn't you?" I asked, even as I tried to restrain myself from touching Sol again. My hands did not seem inclined to listen, and I noticed that she was subtly raising her arm towards the waistband of my hoodie once more.

Gwen fixed me with a glare.

"Some of us have never cared about such things, and I don't keep tabs on all the other gods and their politics. Gods are slow to change, but some of us do. Gaia might be one who does. Or maybe she never cared to begin with. We don't talk much."

"It just doesn't make any sense," said Sol, even as her hand started to slide up under my hoodie once more. I moaned before her hand even reached my breasts, then shook myself and tried to take a step back.

"What. The. Actual. Fuck." I gritted out, through clenched jaws. I wasn't opposed to wanting to jump Sol a bunch in the foreseeable future, but I was trying to hold a conversation, damn it. This was getting ridiculous.

"Ok. For the sake of argument," I managed to say, while stepping back from Sol and her free-roaming hands, "let's say this is a mating bond. How do we get out of it?"

"We don't," said Sol. "Mating bonds are for life. Or… well, that's what I've always heard, anyway."

"But surely no one lives like this?" I said, finding myself sliding towards Sol again, despite not wanting to. "How do they get anything done?"

"It's only supposed to drive people like this until it's completed."

"What do you mean, completed?"

"Consummated."

"Did we, or did we not, just consummate the crap out of each other back there?"

Sol smiled, then forced her hands to her sides.

"We did. If this were a mating bond it should have cooled down by now."

"Not if it isn't just a two person bond," said Gwen gingerly from behind the teakettle that had somehow reassembled itself.

"WHAT?!" Sol and I chorused together.

"That's not possible!" said Sol. "Those bonds are legends, and nothing more."

"You keep using that word. I do not think it means what you think it means."

I couldn't resist putting on my best Iñigo Montoya voice.

Sol was so angry that she ignored my Princess Bride reference completely.

"There hasn't been a three person bond in... I don't know... a thousand years? It's possible it was just a myth to begin with. Why would there be one now? And who would the third be anyway?" Sol looked ready to tear something up, and I was suddenly glad that her hands were no longer under my shirt.

"Um, three person bond, two person bond, why is ANY of this happening? And why us? Why me in particular? I didn't even know this stuff existed."

Sol turned to me and looked like she was finally taking pity on me. "Ok. The short, short version is this: mating pairs feel a very strong pull when they meet each other—the more time they spend together, the more they are drawn in. If they take too "long" getting to know each other without consummating things, they can be thrown into a frenzy until they finally manage to seal the deal. Once they mate properly, they are mated for life. They will always be with that person."

"Why?" I asked.

"Why what?" Sol's eyebrow rose in what I could only assume was confusion.

"Why any of it? Why mate to people for life? Why stay together after the mating bond is consummated? Just... why?"

"Not a believer in monogamy, are you?" Sol asked, smiling.

"Not particularly." I shrugged. "It's not that I don't believe in it. I just have a hard time buying that it's the default switch for most humans. I think the reason most people become dissatisfied with relationships after a few years is a general human tendency towards genetic diversity and thus towards having multiple partners over the long run. Plus, I think it's lame that we try to get *everything* we need in a partner from a single person. No human can reasonably expect to find someone who gives them everything. That's crazy."

Sol's smile widened.

"Well said."

"So, I take it neither of us is thrilled at the idea of being mated for life?" I hedged.

Sol shook her head.

"Gatita, you're hot as fuck, but I do not want to be saddled with you, or anyone else, *forever*."

"Are we having a sharing circle or something?"

Seamus' voice sounded perfectly calm, and perfectly normal, but for some reason it sent a jolt of liquid heat sliding through me.

"Damn," I said, turning to see him standing in the doorway. He was silhouetted by the afternoon light shining over the mountains behind him, and his long, dark hair was pulled back from his angular jawline and high cheekbones. His amber eyes seemed to glow from the doorway, and suddenly I decided he was wearing entirely too much clothing. I'd crossed half the distance between us before I even noticed that my body had moved. I managed to stop myself before I got to him, though.

"What is happening?" I asked, feeling more lost than ever.

"We may have figured out why the earlier consummation didn't take."

I felt another jolt of heat just standing there, watching Seamus as he took off his coat, and was trembling with the effort it took to keep from jumping him where he stood. I'd always found him attractive, but this was ridiculous, and I'd just spent the past hour shagging the life out of Sol.

Once his coat and boots were off, Seamus was standing in front of me. He smelled amazing, like pine trees, rocks, wind, and snow. I caught myself leaning forward to lick his neck, but stopped. He was already leaning down to wrap his arms around me, though.

"What did I miss?" he asked, slowly enveloping my waist with his arms. His breathing and speed suggested each move was calculated. I wondered if he was fighting the same thing Sol and I were.

"Gwen?" I asked.

But Gwen wasn't there.

"Sol?" I tried.

Sol sighed.

"As a were with a theoretical mating bond in place, I should want to tear his throat out for touching you like that," she said, as Seamus' hand starting running up and down my back beneath my hoodie. "But instead, I find myself wanting to watch him take you. And, I have *never* wanted to watch a man have sex before."

Just the idea of it had me pressing myself against Seamus. Poor Seamus; he'd missed all of this. He'd gone for a run, or whatever he'd done, to try to escape this very feeling, and now he was back and everything was just as bad as before, or maybe worse. What the hell must he think of what was going on?

"Is this a mating bond?" Seamus asked, still only caressing my back. I marveled at his restraint. I wanted him to caress so much more than that.

I nodded, trying not to press myself any harder against him.

"Weird," he said. "I always figured it would be between two people of the same animal spirit."

Sol laughed.

"Yeah, and I thought they were never between *three* people."

"But you're the bridge, aren't you?" Seamus asked, his eyes locked on me.

"If you mean am I bisexual?… I think the answer is a resounding yes," I sighed. It was nice to say that out loud finally, and, certainly, if I'd wanted proof here it was. I was just as attracted to Seamus as I had been to Sol. Was still attracted to both of them… was starting to fantasize about being with both of them at the same time…. Of course, sexual attraction was only one part of the whole equation, but for now it was the part that was jumping up and down waving semaphores at me, so I was going to go ahead and let it have its way for a moment.

Sol laughed and came over to stand beside me. She took my arm and Seamus released me on that side, still rubbing his left hand up and down the right side of my back, while Sol grabbed my left arm and pulled me towards the bedroom.

"You're right," he said, looking at her. "I should feel defensive as hell about you touching her like that if this is a mating bond, but…"

His eyes flashed, and I wanted to sprint all three of us to the bedroom.

"You're just picturing me sitting on her face while you ride her, aren't you?" Sol said.

Seamus nodded.

I moaned.

"Can we *please* make that happen? Like right now."

I didn't wait for a reply, I just pulled them both into the bedroom.

HOURS LATER, WHEN none of us could move anymore and we finally decided that we should break for food before we wound up with permanent damage, we emerged, dressed at least partially, into the living room.

I was grateful that no one was out there.

"I'm glad Trevor and Rhelia aren't here at the moment," I said, making my way to the small fridge that was on the far wall of the kitchen. "Do we have ingredients for sandwiches?"

Sol patted me on the back, then hip checked me out of the way so that she had primary access to the fridge.

"Yes. Now, step aside so I can put them together *quickly*. I am fucking starving."

"Me too."

"Me three," agreed Seamus.

I looked at him and smiled.

The three of us had certainly bonded in the past few hours. It was night outside the windows of the cabin and I wondered exactly how many hours we'd spent fucking each other's brains out. The edge had been taken off by that first round, no doubt. As soon as we'd all finished together (and when does that happen to a threesome?) the driving *compulsion* to have my way with Sol and Seamus had all but ceased, but the fun of pleasuring each other so completely had simply made me want more and more each time. Especially when you threw in the novelty of having sex with another woman *and* a man at the same time. I'd fantasized about threesomes before, but since I'd never met a woman I had been attracted to before Sol, I'd never pursued it. Now… Now I couldn't stop pursuing it. Damn. I needed to think about something else, or I was going to drag them both back into the bedroom before we ate. We needed to eat.

"So, do you think the mating bond is… satisfied?" I asked.

Sol looked up from where she was generously applying mayonnaise and mustard to six slices of bread.

"I should fucking hope so," she said.

Seamus cackled.

"Seriously," he agreed.

I smiled.

"I mean it, though," I continued. "Is it going to do that to us again? Because while I'm a huge fan of the results, I do *not* appreciate the means."

Sol and Seamus both nodded.

Then Gwen popped back into existence.

"Oh goody," I said, sighing. "Are you here to answer questions or just raise more of them?"

Gwen frowned.

"Don't you enjoy my visits?" she asked. "My last one was… instructive, wouldn't you say?"

I just glared at her.

She sighed, as though I never appreciated her. She might be right.

"The mating bond is likely satisfied, to answer your question."

"Eavesdrop much?" I asked.

She just shrugged.

Sol shoved a sandwich into my hand, then turned on Gwen.

"Mind telling us what the hell a mating bond is doing on the three of us, anyway? It makes no sense. I'm a lesbian. I don't care how hot it is to watch those two get it on, I am *not* having sex with a man. WHY AM I PART OF A MATING BOND?"

Gwen shook her head.

"I didn't put it on you, if that helps, and I'm not privy to all the details about why it had to be you three, I only know that it does. The whole concept is stupid, if you ask me."

That had all three of us nodding.

"Are we all going to turn batshit nuts whenever either of the others bats their lashes at another person?" I asked. I really couldn't stand jealousy as a concept, and that idea bothered me more than anything.

Gwen snorted. "Not unless you normally would. To my knowledge, the mating bond doesn't make you insane with jealousy unless that's your natural tendency anyway. It just makes you crazily attracted to the person, or people, in the bond."

"What does that mean for Sol and Seamus?" I asked.

"I think Sol just stated pretty clearly what she will and won't do when it comes to Seamus."

"And what if Seamus becomes overwhelmingly attracted to her?"

"He can take care of it with fantasies and his hand?" Gwen said, sounding baffled. "It's not like any of this gives any of you more rights to each other than you would normally grant. Look, I know the traditions around mating bonds go back millennia and are… well, stupidly patriarchal, but the magic behind it is simple enough. It wants to create a bond between certain people that is unbreakable, and that encourages those people to procreate."

All three of us started to object.

"The magic was around before condoms or birth control were a thing, ok?" Gwen raised her hands to forestall our objections as she spoke. "You have every opportunity to prevent pregnancy that anyone else does. The magic just makes you want to screw a bunch, and ok, yeah, it makes you want to stick with people for life, or so I'm told. If you *didn't* have access to birth control, that would greatly increase your chances of reproducing. Since you do… enjoy shagging a lot. Or don't. It's up to you."

I took a deep breath. It was reassuring to hear that we weren't going to be… forced into anything.

"The storytellers always make it sound like the magic of the bond makes people do crazy things to keep each other from 'straying,'" Sol said, still seeming unconvinced.

Gwen smirked.

"The patriarchy is a long-standing, opportunistic, piece-of-shit mythology that has corrupted so much of history, it boggles the mind."

"So… those people were just being jealous assholes?" Sol asked, sounding relieved.

Gwen nodded.

We all three let out a breath I hadn't realized we'd been holding.

I finally took a bite of my sandwich. It tasted heavenly.

Then the door to the cabin exploded in a ball of flames.

"**T**REV! WHAT THE fuck?" I shouted, as Trev fell into the living room fighting with… an unfortunately familiar looking vampire.

Without waiting for any kind of reply or explanation, I jumped into the fight, wondering why Trev was bothering to fight Edik in human form, and what had blown down the door if Trev wasn't a fiery phoenix at the moment.

The answer rapidly became clear as more spells slammed into the cabin, some making their way through the door and singeing past Trev and I, as we grappled with Edik on the floor.

"Hijo de puta!" Sol shouted. "The fucker led them right to us!"

It was the last thing she said before shifting into her panther form and charging at the first MOME agent to stick his head in past the door.

I didn't have time to pay attention to what Sol was doing, I was too busy trying to keep Edik from hurting my brother.

Why aren't you in phoenix form? I asked him, while I struggled to pin Edik down.

They have a null out there. He touched me just as I was about to immolate this asshole.

I didn't know what a null was in the real world, but in most of the fantasy books I read it was someone who absorbed magic. That made sense with what Trev had just described, and I didn't have time to ask for clarification anyway, because Edik was actually fighting me for once, and the asshat was surprisingly fast. It seemed that whatever creepy romantic notion had kept him from attacking me before had expired. Thank Gwen. I needed him to be distracted by me, because Trev was clearly in no shape to fight for much longer, and I wondered if getting hit by a null was the only thing that had happened to him.

How many MOME agents are out there? I asked, while blocking an insanely fast series of punches of from Edik. Not for the first time, I was sincerely glad that Edik didn't seem to have ever trained in a martial art. Even with the way he telegraphed every single one of his punches, kicks, and attempted bites, his moves were almost too fast to track.

Twenty or so, Trev replied. *Rhelia's keeping most of them busy.*

Well fuck. That was a lot of MOME to fight off when one of our most effective fighters couldn't pull on any of his magic. And of course, we were too spread out for me to grab all of us.

Well, if I couldn't get all of us to safety right away, at least I could start taking out the trash.

The next time Edik threw a punch at me, I didn't block it, I just grabbed his fist.

I shifted us all the way back to the school pool in Flagstaff, but I didn't even give him a chance to get his bearings, I just jumped back from him, laughed at the ridiculous expression on his face as he hit the water, and then shifted myself right back to the inside of Sol's cabin.

Luckily, Sol and Seamus had been successful in keeping more MOME agents from gaining access to the house. Trev looked like he was still catching his breath when I grabbed his wrist, before launching myself at Sol and Seamus. They were fighting the nearest MOME agents coming through the doorway.

As soon as I grabbed hold of them, I shifted us to the top of the rise outside of Sol's cabin, hoping that it would be behind enemy lines.

Rhelia! I shouted mentally, hoping to gain the dragon's attention without bringing any more MOME agents to us. Apparently, Sol had been mid-bite to the wrist of a MOME agent when I'd shifted us, because he had come along for the ride, so Sol continued to fight him atop the rocky outcropping that stood 200 meters above her small mountain sanctuary. I joined her, hoping against hope that Rhelia would make her way to us before any of the other MOME agents did. Sol was limping and Seamus was shaking like a leaf, and I remembered that none of us had gotten much sleep or food in the past few days. The best we'd managed was to shag for a few hours and eat a bite of sandwich. We were all running on empty, and Trev looked like he'd run a marathon or something just in order to get here.

Sol must have decided that we were running out of time too, because she lunged for the mage's throat and the man didn't even have time to scream, though he did manage to light Sol's fur on fire as they both went down in a heap together. Not waiting to see if the man was dead, I reached forward and grabbed his arm, shifting him back to the cabin, which was now more of a smoldering hovel than anything else, as the myriad spells that MOME had launched combined with what must have been dragon breath and brought the house most of the way to the ground. I dropped the offending MOME agent in the flaming confines of the living room before shifting myself back to Sol, Seamus, and Trev. Seamus, now in wolf form, leapt to my side and pressed his head against my leg as soon as I appeared.

A roar like a typhoon shook the earth around us, and then we were all knocked to our asses as Rhelia backwinged herself to a spot a few meters above us on the slope. I was almost completely out of energy, but I could hear MOME agents calling to one another from below us. We didn't have time to climb the 200 meters to Rhelia, not in the state we were in. Not with Trev unable to shift.

"To me!" I shouted, feeling a bit like Aragorn, or Gandalf.

Luckily, cheesy one-liners aside, everyone got up and put a hand, snout, or paw against me.

I shifted us to Rhelia's back, and hoped to hell she wouldn't be offended.

If she was upset with me, she gave no indication, instead launching herself skyward while we all still scrambled to find something to hold onto that would keep us from falling to the earth.

Relief coursed through me as she took us higher and higher, and I realized I wouldn't have to shift us all again.

Then I passed out.

I REGAINED CONSCIOUSNESS fighting off an attack from some evil, furred beast that was trying to smother me.

Or… Sol's tail.

I sat up gasping, swatting the offending appendage away from my mouth. Sol and Seamus were curled protectively around me, both asleep. Sol's tail was just doing its own thing. My hands pressed into the sand underneath me, and my eyes finally took in my surroundings. Aquamarine water and white sand took up my field of vision, the water extending all the way to the horizon, until the sky bled into the sea.

"Where are we?" I muttered.

"Ssssomewhere near Fiji," Rhelia's voice called, from behind me. I turned to see her sitting on the beach a little ways behind me, with Trev beside her. They were holding hands.

"Fiji? Holy crap, how long was I out?" I asked.

"Only about a day," Trev replied. Something in his voice made me look him in the eyes, and I realized that he looked wrecked.

"When was the last time you got any sleep?"

He smiled. "I slept most of the way here."

"Then why do you look like shit?"

"Vic, I—"

"Can someone tell me *why* we're in the middle of the Pacific Ocean?" Sol had apparently been woken by our conversation and resumed her human form. She was clothed in a sarong wrapped over a skimpy looking swim suit, and I had to wonder if my Gwen-given powers were pranksters, or if my subconscious had some sway in how everyone wound up clothed. Then I shook myself out of my pondering, because everyone else was still talking.

"MOME are behind us at every turn," Trev grumbled. "Rhelia thought the safest way to lose them was to fly over the ocean for a long assed time."

That made some amount of sense…

"And?" I asked, sensing that we weren't getting the full answer.

"And Rhelia talked to a seer before we left."

As if that was an explanation.

"Just wondering what your next lotto numbers should be?" I asked, giving Rhelia a hard stare.

"The sssseer came to me, actually," Rhelia said. "She gave me a very cryptic messsssage about finding answerssss in the ocean."

"Well, that's pretty vague."

"Indeed," Rhelia agreed. "When I ssssaid asssss much to her, she showed me an image of an island, thissss island, I think."

"Did she show you a map? How did you know where to go?"

"No. Thisssss island issss on no map."

"Well, then how did you—"

"Vic." Trev cut me off. "You didn't finish your initiation ceremony, so there's a lot we can't tell you yet, especially with two people who aren't dragonkin present. Can you just trust us for a minute?"

"So *you* know what's going on here?" I asked, suddenly a bit peeved at all the dragon secrecy shit.

"Not exactly, but I have a better idea of *why* we might be left in the dark about a few things, and yes, it's annoying, but it's mostly with good reason. Besides, if the vague prophecy was in any way accurate, we're about to get a few answers."

I thought about that for a moment, and then something else occurred to me.

"Where the fuck is Albert?" I asked.

"The old mage?" Trev asked.

"Yeah, I haven't seen him since we hit the streets in Unterberg. Have you?"

Seamus must have woken up not long after Sol, because he shifted to human form and said, "He was with us when we moved the MOME refugees to the dragon realm, but he chose not to come back with us. He said he wanted an audience with the circle of elders."

"Hmm… I hope he's as trustworthy as he seems," I muttered.

Rhelia laughed.

"If he issss not, he will be little more than a char mark when nexsssst we return to the elder cssss-sircle."

"Right. I suppose the elders can take care of themselves."

"That issss putting it mildly," Rhelia replied.

"So, how exactly is this island meant to give us answers?" I asked.

Rhelia and Trev got very quiet for a moment, and then Trev stood up.

"Come on, Vic. Follow me."

DRAGONS ARE SNEAKY bastards.

Ok. That's an unfair generalization. The seer who approached Rhelia appeared to have been a sneaky bastard. Minus the slur on her parentage, which I knew nothing about. Still, I was beginning to understand why Trev still looked like a train had hit him, even after a full night's sleep. We hadn't even gotten to where he was leading me yet, and I was already a wreck.

Not as much of a wreck as my parents' boat was, though.

Trev had led me through a small stand of palms that reached almost all the way to the water, then onto a long stretch of beach that was completely empty, save for the small husk of a wrecked yacht. A fifty-footer. The mast was gone, no trace of it left but a gaping hole into the galley beneath where it had once stood.

I glanced at Trev, saw the haunting shadows in his eyes, and realized that he'd probably already had a look around.

The whole mass of wood and fiberglass was sun-bleached and deteriorating, as one might expect from something that had probably washed up on this shore months ago, but it seemed oddly at peace; as though it belonged here on this beach, away from everything else in the world, as though it were simply resting after a job well done.

Ok. Maybe my emotions *were* more of a wreck than the boat.

The name was still visible on the stern. The Victor. I had always hated that name, as much as I'd loved the boat itself. My dad had always assured me it wasn't named for me, especially after I had asked him if he'd wished that I had been born a boy. Mixed feeling about the fading name aside, this boat had been my home every summer since I'd turned seven. The place we'd always escaped to when the requirements of school had released me, and my parents had set aside time for all of us to head to the west coast, climb aboard The Victor, and become floating nomads, kings of our own tiny realm for six weeks out of every year.

I didn't bother to swipe at the tears running down my face as I took a few steps towards what was left of my childhood playground.

Trevor put a hand on my shoulder.

"Vic… you don't have to—"

"Yeah. I do, actually."

I gave Trev's hand a squeeze before I pushed it off of my shoulder, stepping towards the wreckage.

Trevor had been on that boat as a kid, I was sure. The memories that had been leaking, and sometimes flooding, back into my brain since Sol had initially helped me break whatever spell had tried to cut Trevor out of my life confirmed that much, but my parents had just purchased it before Trevor was taken. I don't even think we'd had a chance to do more than resurface the top deck before MOME had snatched him away from us. Perhaps that was part of why the boat had become such a big part of our lives afterwards. It wasn't laden with memories of the twin who had disappeared, the child erased from my parents memories in an attempt to spare the last child they had left. Or maybe we spent so much time there simply because it was a project my parents could obsess over, distract themselves with in an attempt to erase the nagging memories that must have been pulling at them, despite the spells that had tried to erase a quarter of our little family from their hearts.

For me, this boat had almost been another sibling. A playmate that filled a hole I knew was there, but had been convinced was only a figment of my imagination.

Just as I drew level with the boat, I felt a familiar presence at my side.

"Thought you might want some backup," Seamus said quietly.

"You worried the Kraken is going to jump out of this thing?" I asked, unable to keep the exasperation out of my voice, even around the tears. Seamus' protective streak was not something I appreciated.

"Nah. Just ghosts."

"Ghosts can't hurt me, Seamus."

"Lucky you," he snorted. "They manage to hurt the rest of us easily enough."

I turned to look at him then, and when I saw his eyes I no longer wondered why Seamus had come to offer comfort instead of Sol or Trevor. The shadows that haunted Seamus' eyes made me reach out to wrap an arm around him.

"One of these days, when no one is trying to kill us, I really need to ask you more about yourself, don't I?"

Seamus leaned into the one-armed embrace, still facing the boat, while I tucked my head into his shoulder.

"Meh. We'll get to it eventually. It's been a busy week. Some things are not exactly at the top of my list of things to talk about, even when no one is trying to kill me." He shrugged.

I chuckled, but the sound didn't hold much humor.

"Yeah. These things aren't my favorite conversation pieces either," I said, nodding towards the boat that had likely been my parents pallbearer. "Still, you shouldn't remain all dark and mysterious just because I've been too self-absorbed to ask you any questions."

"Don't be too hard on yourself, Vic. I'm not much of a talker."

I sighed.

"We doing this?" I asked.

He nodded.

I stepped forward, my right arm still loosely wrapped around Seamus' torso.

I stood before the hole in the galley where the mast had once been, the wooden deck lying almost perpendicular to the beach. I doubted much of the keel was left, but whatever was there was likely ensuring that the boat stayed on its side.

My left hand reached out to the deck, and I could feel the salt drying on my cheeks where the sun was evaporating the tracks of my tears. The sound of the turquoise ocean around us faded, the scenery of this tiny island paradise all but disappearing, as I refocused my attention on the miniature floating world that had once been my home away from home. Even the faded grain of the wood was familiar enough to be a blow to the gut. Gwen knows I'd sanded it enough times, I'd probably recognize it with my eyes closed.

When my hand connected with the deck I felt as though I'd touched a live wire. I tried to jump back and let go of Seamus, convinced that some of the navigation equipment must have managed to electrify the timbers of the deck, but I couldn't move an inch. My arm went rigid and my jaw locked tight, preventing me from even screaming. My eyes rolled into my head, and a series of images, worse than even my most devastating nightmares, cascaded across my vision.

My parents, crying, hugging each other as they watched The Victor sink beneath a violent sea from the dubious vantage of a small motor boat that looked likely to be overcome by the thrashing waves that surrounded them. A man I'd never seen before, with bulging eyes and prominent fangs, pounding against a locked door, rattling the windows and screeching, a half-dozen children huddled crying on the other side as the hinges shook. A wolf, torn limb from limb in a way that no natural predator would ever have left it. A young boy, drawing a picture of that same wolf, and a redheaded woman, tearing the picture into shreds. Six men and women sneaking up on a small wooden cabin under cover of darkness, wands drawn and guns out. Two women in pajamas screaming, turning into wolves and being hit with multiple spells and bullets, eventually falling still.

Suddenly, I was lying in the sand looking up at three sets of legs.

"Seamus?" I asked, hoping he was as not dead as I was.

"I'm ok."

"What the hell was that, Seamus?"

"We have to go, Vic."

"What the HELL was that?"

"Vic, we have to go. We have to get back to Flagstaff!"

"I'm not going anywhere until you tell me what that was!"

"There isn't time, Vic!"

"Fucking make time! What did I just see?!"

"I don't know what triggered it. That's never happened to me before. I saw *your* parents and then I saw… things I've seen before."

"You can start making sense any time now."

I was grateful that the owners of all the feet that surrounded us were staying out of it, for now— maybe because Seamus and I were both clearly alive and conscious. I supposed no one else was shouting questions at Seamus because no one else had just seen a vision of the last moments of their parents' lives followed by… whatever all that other shit was.

"I see the future sometimes, Vic. Sometimes the past, I guess. But mostly that's just me reliving visions I've already had, or nightmares of things I already lived through. The future though… you can understand why I don't talk about it, right? Almost no one believes in seers, Vic. Not even in our world. I was amazed to hear Rhelia talk about what she heard from a seer without a hint of derision in her voice. I guess dragons have their own thing going on, but for humans, mages, weres… it's not like there haven't been a few throughout history, but… it's not a healthy condition, right? People kill you for what you do see, or what you don't see, or what you *might* see. It's not something you go around mentioning to folks, if you want to die of old age. My family doesn't even really believe it—the few who even know about it. Did you… did you see all of that?"

I nodded, too stunned to speak for a moment.

"I don't know if we saw the same things, but… I saw a kid who drew a picture of a wolf torn limb from limb… was that you?"

"Sometimes the visions come when I'm drawing, especially when I was younger, but mostly they come as dreams. They don't come often, regardless, but… Vic, we have to go. My moms. My moms are in danger. That vision. The mages closing in on that cabin. That's my house, Vic. I had that vision for the first time a month before I met you, but it was different the first time. The first time I had it *you* were there. And you saved them. You saved my moms' lives and… they're all I've got, Vic. Please."

Holy fucking shitballs, Seamus was begging me to save his parents. What kind of friend was I? Did he really think he'd have to *convince* me to help him save his family? Even if I was a little worried that he'd only befriended me to ensure I was around to help him, I wasn't going to say no to doing whatever I could to save his moms.

Trev, stay here and find out what is up with this Gwen-damned boat.

Then I grabbed Seamus' hand and shifted us the hell to Flagstaff.

THE WOODS OUTSIDE of Seamus' cabin were dark, thanks to being on the opposite side of the world from Fiji. I had been forced to shift us to my place first, very briefly, since I had never been to Seamus' home before, and he'd tried calling his moms to warn them about the possibly impending attack, while I had run upstairs to grab something. There had been no answer at his place.

We hadn't waited after that, I'd just had him bring up a few images of his home on his phone, then I'd reached through space and time and deposited our asses into the middle of the woods 100 meters from the house.

I'd decided that inside a house that might be crawling with evil mages wasn't a good place to appear all of a sudden. Or at all, preferably.

From our vantage point, the house looked calm enough. There was no sign of any disturbance. The porch light glowed welcomingly, but the interior lights were off.

"Could they be asleep?" I asked.

Seamus checked his phone.

"It's 7:30. Not likely."

I nodded.

"Out to dinner?"

"Maybe," he replied. He did not sound convinced.

I kept my eyes on the house and the surrounding wilderness, but could see Seamus texting someone, out of the corner of my eye.

"They're not at Uncle Rom's," he said, after a minute.

That didn't sound like good news.

Just then, a light flicked on in the window of the cabin, and a silhouette briefly blocked out the light that was seeping out between a set of dark curtains.

"Was that either of your mothers?" I asked, fairly sure of the answer due to the dropping feeling in my gut, and the fact that the silhouette had looked pretty much like a dude.

"No." Seamus' voice sounded cold. I reached out my hand and squeezed his.

"Plan B?" I asked.

He nodded, squeezing my hand in return.

I shifted us again.

~~~

"Ow! Fuck!" I whispered angrily, as my head made contact with a low beam.

"Shhh!" Seamus admonished.

In my defense, I had barely vocalized the sentiment, though my head was now throbbing with the impact. If the stooges upstairs weren't weres, then there was no way that they could have heard me, and even if they were, it was was unlikely unless they were already in their animal forms.

This basement was not made for human habitation, and it wasn't just the goose egg on my forehead that proved it. The spiderwebs I was working hard not to inhale were further evidence, along with whatever squishiness was making my boots sink into the... ground? Dead rats? What the hell was I standing on?

"They should be here by now."

Seamus and I stiffened. The voice came from directly above us, muffled by the flooring and insulation that separated us from his moms' bedroom.
~~~

I looked at Seamus, but it was clear from the cold rage suffusing his face that the voice had not belonged to someone in his family.

"How many times do we have to tell you—he isn't here, and he isn't coming! He's traveling with friends, and he's too smart for whatever ridiculous trap you—."

The sound of flesh connecting with flesh resounded above us, and I put my hand on Seamus' arm, worried that he might do something rash… like tear through the floor and launch himself at whoever had clearly just hit one of his moms.

I looked at him, and with the diffuse light that seeped in, I could see his lips pulled back in a silent snarl that very effectively imitated his wolf form.

I wished I could communicate with him the way that Trevor and I did. Anything to try to help calm him. Now was not the time to lose our shit, though I couldn't blame him for the impulse at all.

"Whatever you assholes did to keep us from shifting to wolf isn't going to be enough to keep me from killing you all at the end of this."

That was uttered by a different female voice, one that I thought sounded a bit like a slightly higher version of Seamus'.

But as soon as I processed the meaning of the words, I grabbed Seamus' arm more forcefully and pulled us back to the far corner of the basement instead of worrying about who had spoken them.

Seamus resisted at first, but soon realized where I was headed and probably assumed I was just taking him to the corner so that we could whisper out a plan with less chance of being overheard.

Instead, as soon as we were as close to the wall as I could get us, I pulled on time and space and dropped us in the woods outside the house once more. Only this time it felt like I had to reach through a wall of taffy to find the power that had come so easily to me only minutes before.

"What the HELL, VIC!" Seamus turned on me, teeth bared, as soon as we had fully materialized in the woods.

"Are nulls a real thing?" I asked, stepping back from him, hoping to lead him deeper into the woods in case he decided to yell any louder and let all the damned mages in the world know that we were here.

"What?!"

"Nulls. People, or devices, that absorb magic and keep spells and shit from happening. They exist in half the fantasy books I read. Do they exist in real life? Trev said he was touched by one back in Bolivia and then he couldn't shift."

Seamus thought about that for a long moment.

"They might exist. I don't know any personally, and they would probably be mages, or related to them, but I've heard a story or two with a person that fit that description."

I nodded.

"Well, I think that the mages in your parents' place have brought one along for the ride. One of your moms was talking about not being able to shift, and pulling us out here felt like pulling through a wall of taffy just now, when pulling us in five minutes ago felt as easy as any other shift."

"Couldn't you just be getting tired? You brought us here from Fiji, after all."

"Yeah, but the distance shouldn't matter. If I'm wrinkling time and space to bring two points together, the distance between doesn't matter. The thing that tires me out is doing it over and over again, or taking multiple people on multiple rides. So far I've only brought you on two, now three, trips, while being fairly well rested, although I'll admit I'm damned hungry."

"Here," he said, handing me an energy bar that he pulled from the cargo pocket on his snow pants, leaving me reeling at how quickly he'd transitioned from wanting to kill me for taking him away from his moms to worrying about my well-being.

"I'm sorry I took you away from your folks," I said, biting into the slab of crunchy peanut butter energy bar. "I didn't know where the null was, or if we'd be able to get out of there, or pull on were forms at all if we stayed. It didn't seem like a good idea to walk into that kind of trap without some kind of backup."

"What kind of backup is going to help us when our magic won't work at all?"

"This," I said, holding up the Glock 45 I'd retrieved from beneath a floorboard under my bed.

"I thought you hated guns," Seamus said, grimacing at the handgun I was holding up.

"I do," I said, loading it and stuffing two extra clips into my pockets. "But an ex of mine loved guns, taught me how to shoot, and bought me this thing for Christmas one year."

"And you kept it?"

I shrugged.

"After my parents died and I started living alone, it seemed like a not terrible idea for a bit… but I locked it up with the ammo stored in a separate container, so… not actually all that useful for home defense."

"Why didn't you use that on Edik?"

I shrugged.

"I didn't really expect him to show up, so it's not like I could have gotten the gun loaded fast enough to be useful. And I really wasn't lying—I do hate guns. But we both saw the vision. The assholes in there are going to try to kill your moms, or us, or both, and we can't use magic against them. Of course, that should mean they can't use magic against us, either."

"Which means that they probably have guns too."

I nodded. "Shitty, but better than taking a pointy stick to a gun fight."

Seamus sighed.

He held up his phone and swiped to the lock screen. On it was a photo of two happy-looking women hugging a slightly bashful-looking Seamus in wolf form. One of them looked just like him, but thinner, and with shorter hair. The other was much paler, with freckled skin and long, curly red hair.

I smiled.

"Alexandra is the redhead, Rowan is the one who shares my dashing good looks. Don't shoot either of them, ok?" he said, sounding stern.

I nodded.

"Definitely not."

Then I thumbed off the safety with my right hand, grabbed his hand with my left, and shifted us both to his front porch.

~~~

"Open up, douchetarts, or I come in shooting," I shouted, raising my Glock to chest level on the door and shoving Seamus behind me.

"How did they—"

"SILENCE!"

Both those voices had come from inside. Oh good. Dissension among the ranks, perhaps? That might help us out.

When the door popped open, I had my gun trained straight at the chest of a six-foot-tall man who was holding one of the women Seamus had just showed me on his cell phone homescreen by the throat, with a gun leveled at her temple.

It was incredibly tempting to aim high and put a hole in the pale douchetart's forehead, but I didn't want to risk giving him enough time to shoot Rowan. Which meant that we were at a bit of an impasse.

Luckily, he seemed to come from the Bond School of Villainy. He was feeling chatty.
~~~

"You shouldn't play with guns, little girl," the man said, condescension dripping from his voice as he gestured at me with his 9mm.

As soon as he pulled the barrel away from Rowan's head, I pulled the trigger. I didn't aim at his forehead, tempting though it had been. I shot him straight in the chest. Center of mass, so even if I didn't hit his heart, I would likely pierce a lung or something. I wasn't really trying to kill him, though that was a likely outcome, but I needed him down and I wasn't willing to risk him shooting any of the people I cared about, myself included.

He clearly hadn't been expecting me to pull the trigger. He didn't return fire. No surprise there. The 9mm he had been holding slid from his hand and he clutched at the newly created hole in his chest, blood seeping past his fingers. His body dropped to the floor in counterpoint to the bile rising in my throat.

I wasted no time stepping forward and using my foot to push the 9mm behind me, towards Seamus, while also pulling Seamus' mom clear of the doorway. I managed not to puke while I did it, but barely.

This is why I fucking hate guns. They are not for screwing around. Mages apparently didn't respect them properly. Or this guy hadn't. You don't wave guns around to try to get your way when you don't know how to use them, or when you think you'll just intimidate someone else who is also armed.

"Anyone else?" I said, gun still raised, finger resting on the trigger guard, stepping forward so that I blocked line of sight from the cabin to both Seamus and Rowan. I could hear her sobbing loudly, but she wasn't screaming, and she hadn't thrown up yet. I was thankful for that. If she threw up, I was certain I would too.

The remaining people in the room were all in various stages of shock, as the tall mage I'd shot lay bleeding, now unconscious, across the threshold. He must have been the one in charge, because no one else seemed inclined to step up.

I quickly assessed the room. There were five more mages, and one woman who matched the other one in the photo on Seamus' phone. They all seemed to be unarmed. Even the woman who was restraining Alexandra didn't seem to have a weapon on her. Perhaps she was the null.

"Anyone else have a gun they want to wave about? Anyone else not understand how easy it is for me to kill you with this?"

I didn't gesture wildly about the room, but I kept the gun up and ready, my finger on the trigger guard, the safety still off.

I was starting to get angry. It might have been the shock of just having shot someone, or rage that I had needed to shoot someone in order to protect people I cared about, or it could have been the fact that this was yet more evidence that MOME didn't give a fuck about justice, and only cared about eliminating threats to its own power. Also, MOME allowed complete douchetarts to lead missions that involved abducting civilians, and Gwendamnit, I really needed to take a few deep breaths before I started to shoot holes in the wall.

"Your null is canceling whatever shields you might normally have against bullets, and on top of that, you can't even fight back with magic right now. We have all the guns, and you have nothing, so I suggest you give me Alexandra there, and I will put this damned thing away so we can all just get back to our lives. If you hurry, you may even have a chance to keep Captain Asshat here from bleeding to death."

No one moved.

"Fine. Alexandra, can you walk?" I asked.

She paled, but nodded and began to stand.

"If anyone but Alexandra moves, I will shoot them," I added, just for good measure.

No one else moved.

See? When you prove up front that you are a) capable of, and b) willing to, shoot someone, people don't fuck around. If you're not willing to shoot someone, don't wave a gun around. Coercion with a gun certainly can work, since enough people are terrified of them, especially if they themselves are unarmed, but then there are the *other* people carrying guns who will just shoot you the moment you hesitate. And in a state like Arizona, where a five-year-old can basically buy an Uzi, why would you risk it?

It seemed like it took Alexandra an hour to cross the small hardwood floor between where she had been held to where the barely breathing body of the man who had opened the door now lay. Without lowering the gun or looking away from the five remaining mages, I sidestepped, so that she could climb over Captain Asshat and out the door.

"I really wish you assholes would just leave me and my family alone," I said, backing myself carefully out over the too-still body of Captain Asshat and onto the front porch. I closed the door, which thankfully had remained unblocked, and finally lowered the gun, putting the safety on. Then I wiped the tears from my face.

"Hold on tight," I said, wrapping Seamus and his moms in a bear hug, after tucking the gun into the holster I'd worn to bring it here. I might have imagined it, but I thought all three of them grimaced slightly when I touched them. I couldn't really blame them, but it still hurt.

I tried to ignore the wretched feeling in my stomach, and reached through time and space for the one thing in the universe that still felt like home.

"**T**REV?"

I must have fainted after I shifted everyone back to that tiny island near Fiji, but sure enough, the thing that had drawn me there swayed gently in front of my eyes.

"You dead, Numo?" Trev asked, his golden eyes dancing in the sunlight, the cerulean sky behind him clear as crystal.

"Yep."

"Well, too bad. I need you in this world."

I smiled, and was pleased to note that it didn't hurt to do so. Nor did it hurt to breathe in the salt-scented air that caressed us. In fact, I just felt a bit tired and mildly sore, like I'd gone for an extra long trail run the day before, on a steeper than usual mountain.

"Is everyone else here?" I asked, deciding it was safe to maybe sit up.

Trev nodded. "Seamus and his moms are over by the fire with Sol."

"A fire in the middle of the day?" I asked, taking another look at the sun glittering off the waves that crashed against the white sand shore stretching away from us in both directions.

"It seemed like a nice enough distraction." Trev shrugged.

"Is everyone ok?"

"They seem pretty shaken, but mostly alright. How are *you*?"

I really didn't want to answer that question, and wasn't sure what to say anyway, so I decided to go with a change of subject. "Any luck with Mom and Dad's boat?"

Trev was sitting on the sand beside me, the lines of concern on his face receding somewhat when I managed to keep my balance while sitting.

"Negative," he replied, sighing. "I don't know what it was supposed to tell us, besides the fact that Seamus' moms were in trouble, but that seems like something he might have gotten a vision about anywhere... doesn't really seem to me like 'answers.'"

"Yeah. That'd be a stretch even for a prophecy, I'd think. We could ask Seamus..." I hesitated.

"Maybe you could ask Seamus if that makes sense for a message from a seer."

Trev quirked an eyebrow at me.

"Why wouldn't *you* ask Seamus?"

I sighed and closed my eyes, not feeling brave enough to watch Trev's face while I confessed.

"Because I don't know if he wants to talk to me anymore, after seeing me shoot someone in the chest."

You don't have to hide from me, Vic. I've done a few things I'm not terribly proud of in order to keep MOME from hurting people.

When I opened my eyes and dared a look at his face, he looked sincere, and sounded it too, as he continued, "I know it probably makes you sick, and that's fine. That's healthy, but… it's not your fault that MOME forced you into violence to protect yourself."

"Isn't it, though?" I asked, my voice a bit desperate. "Couldn't I have talked them into handing over Seamus' moms? Offered myself in exchange? Something? What if I hadn't taken a gun with me?"

"If you hadn't taken a gun with you, you would either all be captured by MOME right now, or Seamus' moms would be dead. There's no way that MOME would have negotiated with you and held up their end of the deal. They either would have harmed Seamus' family anyway, or they would have kept you all prisoner."

"And is that so bad? What if we were all prisoners? How bad would that be? At least no one would be dead."

Apparently, my unconscious mind had been hard at work on drumming up all the toughest questions while I was passed out. I wanted to agree with Trev. I wanted to be angry with MOME, hell I *was* angry with them. I was furious with the asshole I'd shot, because he'd made it seem like the only sensible option in a deadly situation… but I was still sure that it was wrong. That if I were a better person, or a more powerful shifter, or *something,* I wouldn't have had to shoot that man.

"There is some possibility that he might not have shot anyone. Maybe he would just have locked all four of you up. I think it's a very slim chance, Vic, since he had a gun pointed at Rowan's head, but for argument's sake let's say there was a chance. What then? What happens after you, Seamus, and Seamus' moms are locked up by MOME?"

I shrugged, as my brain just reminded me over and over again that at least I wouldn't have shot anyone in the chest, but Trev just kept talking.

"Do you think that Sol, Rhelia, and I would have just let that slide? Do you think we would have just left you guys in MOME custody to rot, or worse? We would have come after you, Vic. As sure as the sun rises in the morning, we would have come after you. And how many of us would still be standing at the end of that?"

My head was starting to hurt and tears were pouring down my cheeks, so I didn't say anything, just stood up and started walking, not paying attention to where I was going, just walking, away from Trev. Away from everyone else. Away from all the people who hadn't pulled the trigger of a gun that was pointed at someone else's chest a few hours ago.

Of course I wound up in front of Mom and Dad's boat.

Because the universe hates me.

Because I wasn't fucking crying hard enough as it was.

Because dragon seers are sneaky pieces of shit.

Barely able to see through the tears, and feeling like I was going to throw up and faint all at once if I didn't just sit down, I collapsed face-first against the deck, which lay at a forty-five degree angle to the sand. Unable to comfort myself in any way, I cried.

And cried.

And cried some more.

Because sometimes you cry so long you forget why you're crying, so then you think of reasons you might need to cry, and you're suddenly flooded with things, some small—a stupid comment about how 'exotic' you look, some huge—shooting someone in the chest, being assaulted in your own home, your parents dying—that have hurt you in the past year or more, and you just need to keep crying until you sort of mentally go through the entire checklist and start to feel better.

I don't even know how long I'd been there when I heard footsteps in the sand behind me. It seemed like hours, but it might have only been minutes.

"Feel any better?" Trev asked.

I nodded, using the hem of my shirt to wipe some of the snot from my face.

"I think I had been holding that in for a while," I admitted.

Trev stepped closer and I briefly felt his hand rest on my shoulder as he leaned his side against the boat, and—

It was then that a shriek like a dying banshee tore at my ears, and seemed to tear at the very fabric of time and space. It was followed by a deafening clap, like the end note of a lightning strike.

Then our mother stood in front of us, half hidden in the shadows of the galley, with her right arm wrapped around our father. They both looked… pale.

"Hey Vic," my mom said, her voice sounding tired.

"Mom?!" I stuttered, my voice barely audible.

"Hey Trev." This time my mom's voice sounded ready to break. Trev and I both started to take a step forward to reach for our parents, but Mom's voice was urgent.

"Don't let go of the boat!"

We both stopped in our tracks.

"If you're watching this," she said, taking a deep breath, "then we're dead, which sucks, but isn't too surprising in the grand scheme of things. More importantly, it means you two have found each other."

And here she took a moment to wipe away a few tears.

"Which makes all of this worthwhile, if you ask me."

I looked between them both, my mom and dad, *dead*, I'd thought. Dead, she'd just said. But why was I seeing them? Why did it look like they were standing right in front of me? Was it a hologram?

Was it some quirky mage message? What the fuck was going on? And why couldn't I hug my parents?

"Mom," I started, but she just kept on talking, as though I hadn't said anything.

"If you two are back together, then there's literally nothing that MOME can do to us that isn't worth it."

My dad was nodding fervently, but was crying too hard to say anything. I could feel Trev trembling beside me, and I wanted to throw both of my arms around him, but Mom had said not to let go of the boat. Would this message disappear? Would we ever be able to see it again? I couldn't risk it, and I figured Trevor would understand.

"We don't have much time. They've been catching up with us since we left Cape Town and we don't have much longer to try our last gambit, which, if you're watching this, probably didn't work, but who knows. Maybe you'll never see this, or maybe they'll only catch us years from now. There's no guaranteeing that any of this will play out the way we hope it will, even you two seeing this. Maybe especially that. We're counting on Vic's persistence, and MOME's greed, and hoping beyond hope that Trev… Trev, that they left something of you in there, that they didn't erase our sweet mischievous boy…. You're so much smarter than they are, sweetie. We just have to hope that you remember it at all the most important times."

She stopped to wipe her nose and eyes. Dad had already hidden his face in her shoulder.

"I'm rambling," she said, taking another deep breath. "You need to know the truth. Both of you. It'll have to be the Cliff's Notes, I'm afraid, because this storm is picking up and we have to get going, but… they're after us because of what we know. Because we know what they're planning to do, and how they're planning to do it. It's…"

A loud thud sounded on the hull, and my parents both looked at each other.

"Gods damn it!" my mom shouted. "It's an army, Vic. Trevor will likely understand exactly what kind of army, and even how they're making it. It's why they took him. Vic, it's an army of people like you and Trevor. Like me and your dad. They're using all the misfits of the magical world and training them, but they're not training them to help them, they're training them to use them. We think—damn it!"

There was another large noise in the background, and my dad hugged my mom furiously, gave her one kiss, turned towards us and said, "I love you both, and I always have."

Then he turned his tear-streaked face towards whatever lay behind him, disappearing from sight.

"They're here. That's not just the storm anymore. We have to go," my mom continued, tears rising to her eyes. "We suspect that they're also preparing a weapon, but we don't have proof."

She turned to me then, and it felt like she was looking straight into my soul, even though this was by all appearances some kind of recording.

"Vic, you need to find my journals. I can't say more than that, in case… just find them. They'll tell you everything you need to know."

Then she turned and looked to where Trevor was standing beside me, and I could only assume she pierced him with the same stare she'd just used on me.

"Trevor, you could be the key to stopping all of this. With all that you've probably learned… Teach Vic. Teach her everything. Between the two of you, you can make sure this doesn't happen to anyone else. Families shouldn't be torn apart like this, and MOME shouldn't get to take over the world."

She paused, as though listening to something, but whatever it was, I couldn't hear it.

"I love you both," she said, baring a watery smile. "Give 'em hell."

Then she turned and was gone.

Trev and I just stood there, silent and unmoving, for a long, long time, and then one more long time, just for good measure. One of us was shaking, but I wasn't sure which one. Maybe it was both of us.

"How did they know we would find each other?" I asked eventually, still standing with my hand awkwardly against the hull, Trevor beside me, matching my pose.

"How did they know we would find the boat?" Trev asked.

"How did they make that recording? That felt like they were here. I felt like I could have touched them."

"Ghosts," Trevor said.

"What? You're telling me those were their spirits? Are they haunting the boat?"

"No. Well, sort of. They're not haunting it. It was just a message. And it's not their spirits, or not the whole of their spirits anyway. They left remnants of themselves here to deliver the message."

"Remnants? Do you mean they left a portion of their souls here? How does that work? Wouldn't that kill you? Or fundamentally change you? How can anyone do that?"

"It's not recommended, but if you're about to die anyway…"

Right. Intentionally shear off a portion of your soul to deliver a message, instead of risk dying with something important unsaid. Fair enough, I could imagine a few scenarios dire enough to warrant that, and this one certainly counted, but…

"I may be clinging to my Potter lore a little too hard here, but wouldn't that be the kind of thing the bad guys teach you?"

Trev shrugged.

"Maybe. If the bad guys are MOME? Probably. They're more about practicality, and you have to admit it has its uses. Even some old failing countess or whatever could use it to will stuff to people if she needed to, right? I mean, it's not like you're shearing off a part of someone else's soul."

"But wouldn't the principle be the same? I mean if you can shear off some of your own soul, couldn't you shear off someone else's… fuck, why am I clinging to this? It doesn't matter." I took a deep breath. "Was that really our parents, Trev?"

"I think so, Vic. That kind of thing is pretty hard to fake."

And that was when I started to cry.

I think Trev joined me, but I never was sure.

The boat burst into flames before I had a chance to get a good look.

"**W**OULD IT BE too much to ask that you NOT immolate the last vestige of our dead parents?" I asked, jumping back from the now-flaming wreckage.

"That is *not* me," Trev said. He was looking frantic, and also seemed to be straining, like he was trying to do advanced calculus while taking a shit. "It's not responding to any of my magic!"

I looked all around us, desperate to find a way to stop the flames. The ocean was only a few meters away, but it might as well have been a thousand miles, for all the good it did us without even a bucket to move it.

"Rhelia!" Trev shouted, and I could hear the call inside my mind as well.

She must have been close by; I heard the wing-beats before I saw the dragon herself, and she lay down on top of the boat as though hoping to smother the flames.

Then she hissed and shot skyward again.

It will not bend to my will and is too hot for my scales, she sent, before flapping the short distance to the ocean and squelching whatever bits of fire had adhered to her.

And before we could even look for another method of putting out the flames, the conflagration roared even higher, then suddenly stopped.

Apparently it had run out of fuel.

There was nothing left of my parents' old boat but a few charred coals.

"Gwendamnit! Can't a few hours pass without something *completely* shitty happening to us?!" I shouted at the cloudless sky.

Sol must have walked over while I was too pre-occupied with putting out an impossible fire for me to notice, because suddenly she was right next to my shoulder, saying, "Well, we did have a handful of not-shitty hours yesterday."

Her voice was practically purring, and the reminder of how good things had been that day sent warm shivers coursing over my body.

"Hey, Gatita," she whispered, wrapping me in a hug that left me warm in more ways than one. "Te echaba de menos."

I smiled and breathed in the sun-soaked scent of her skin.

"I missed you too," I murmured, realizing that it was true even as I said it. It was strange to think of how much closer Sol, Seamus, and I were than even a few days ago.

"Rowan and Alexandra were just regaling us with tales of your heroics," she said, not letting me go. "I hope you don't feel too bad about shooting that asshat."

I laughed a little bit, and probably cried a bit too, I don't really remember, but it felt good to be held by someone I was intimate with and not feel rejected for all that I'd done today.

"Now," she said, looking between Trev and me, while still holding me close, "Why exactly did you set your old boat on fire?"

~~~

One hour, and a whole lot of fruitless searching of our tiny island oasis, found us no closer to figuring out why the boat had ignited, except that
~~~

maybe it was set to self-destruct like a secret message in a cheesy spy movie. Which, the way my life had been going lately, seemed just as likely as anything else. Especially when you considered the contents of our parents' final message to us. It wasn't the kind of thing that they'd have wanted MOME to know they knew about. Then again, why was MOME after them to begin with, if not because they knew things they shouldn't? Maybe they were more concerned with MOME finding out that *we* now knew more about their evil schemes.

Sadly, Sol had no answers for us.

"I've only been at MOME for about two years, so I'm not privy to any information about secret armies or secret weapons. I worked my ass off to make it into the special services department just to get higher security clearance, but I still haven't been granted access to anything more than the personal files of people I've been charged with tracking down. You and Trev being prime examples. But even then, I was only given partial access to your file. It's the file you rescued from MOME that has all of the real details, and that was something I never had access to."

"Fuck," I said, just barely restraining myself from slapping my own forehead.

"What?" asked Trev and Sol at once.

"The file. It was in my pack when we left Sol's cabin to go to Unterberg…. I never got it back from the council after they took us."

"Shit. So the Unterberg council is in possession of our family's file?" Trev asked, looking a bit paler than usual.

"Yep."

"What are the chances that they haven't taken a look at it?" Trev asked.

"Not good," Sol replied. "They would be looking for anything they could to incriminate you."

"But they can't touch us now, can they?" I asked. "And besides, what about Mom and Dad's file would they find incriminating, I mean it's not like they—"

"They trained with Albert, Vic. Voluntarily. They sought out instruction from a MOME researcher when they were teenagers. The Unterberg council won't find that very reassuring. They'll assume that they were MOME sympathizers."

"But that doesn't make sense. They all seemed bummed when I made that joke about Dad being dead, which made it seem like they respected him."

"Maybe they hadn't found the file yet when they were talking with us, or maybe they respected him anyway, but regardless it's not a good thing that they have that file in their hands."

"Fine. How do you even know that about Mom and Dad? That they trained with Albert by choice, I mean."

"I must have gotten farther into their file than you did. Plus, I talked to Albert afterwards."

"Talked? More like shouted-at-a-whole-bunch," Sol scoffed.

Trev smiled a bit sheepishly.

"Yeah, well, I was a bit mad at our parents for keeping certain secrets from us, and I may or may not have taken my anger out on Albert."

That made me chuckle.

"Well, as the principal to a public high school, I imagine he's fairly used to that by now. So, what do we do now? I think it's pretty important that we figure out what MOME is up to. The idea that they're training an army," I glanced at Trev, wondering if he knew more about that part than he was letting on, "or building some secret weapon… I mean, it sounds like something out of a Bond movie, but Mom and Dad weren't prone to conspiracy theories… I think."

Trev looked me straight in the eyes, as if he knew what I'd been thinking, and who knows, maybe he did.

"I wouldn't be surprised if some of the kids that were taken by MOME were being trained, or brainwashed or whatever, to be used as an army, and it wouldn't be hard to imagine how powerful an army of kids like us would be, but don't worry Vic, if MOME was trying to make me sympathetic to their side, they failed every time they threatened you or our parents."

Sol looked between us both, shaking her head.

"Twins creep me out sometimes. I feel like you two just had a conversation I couldn't hear."

I laughed.

"That was nothing compared to the actual conversations we have that you can't hear," I said, giving her an exaggerated wink.

"Alright you three," Seamus called from a hundred meters down the beach. He had crossed half the distance between us and where his moms and Rhelia were sitting around a small fire doing... who knew what. "Come talk to the rest of us. We need a plan."

When we made our way to the rest of the group, Seamus smiled at the three of us, and the fact that he included me in the gesture went a long way to easing the hurt I'd felt when we'd first shifted back here.

"We have a very important issue that needs resolving immediately," he said, shifting his face to a more somber expression. "I'm hungry."

Y HOUSE WAS untouched since the last time I'd been there, and it felt a bit surreal to be back within its walls. Somehow, traveling between countries and realms in the blink of an eye, learning that dark matter coursed through my veins, giving me access to a snow leopard form and teleportation, and learning that the world was full of what was still best described as magic, (in my mind at least), had made me feel more out of place than I'd ever felt before. Yet, even so, arriving at the house my parents had left me in their will didn't feel like a homecoming at all. I felt as out of place here now as I had any-where else. It felt like these walls couldn't contain all that had happened to me in the past two weeks.

In the end, we had decided to send Rowan and Alexandra to Unterberg with Rhelia, since they were all unquestionably welcome there still, to see if they could convince the Unterberg council to hand over my family's file and provide a safe place for Rowan and Alexandra to stay until we could be sure that MOME wasn't going to try to kill them in their own home. Unfortunately, at the moment, that seemed likely to be a permanent arrangement. I felt awful that they'd had to leave their home so suddenly, but at least we could be sure that they would have a safe, MOME-free place to hide.

Sol, Seamus, Trev, and I, on the other hand, had decided to listen to Seamus' stomach and head someplace we knew was well-stocked with snacks, not to mention also a potential hiding place for the mysterious journals that my mom had mentioned.

Sol, the self-appointed sandwich-maker-in-chief, had taken on the task of preparing food for us all, while Trev worked on checking the house for sensors, tracking devices, spells, or any other ugly surprises that MOME might have left for us. Since we weren't useful to either of those tasks, Seamus and I, grumbling stomachs and all, started to search the house.

"Hey," Seamus said, after we walked into one of the storage cupboards on the main floor and started opening boxes that looked like they had been here since before I was born, "I just wanted to thank you… for saving my moms."

"Seamus, you know I never would have left you to do that alone, right?"

I turned, still wary of what I might see in Seamus' eyes, but finally willing to face whatever it was… but he was staring determinedly at a half-opened box full of cookbooks.

"That's not what I mean, Vic. I mean… it was really hard for me to see you shoot someone, but… but not harder than it must have been for you to actually do it, and if you hadn't…"

He turned to look at me, finally, and I saw the unshed tears in his eyes.

"He was going to kill them, Vic. I saw it in my visions, over and over again. Every time I had that vision and you weren't there, they died. I thought I would be ok with… with what you had to do, because I'd seen it probably a dozen times in my head by the time it really happened, but… it still shocked me."

He was silent for a long moment, and when I finally reached for him and he didn't flinch at all, I wrapped him in the biggest bear hug I could manage.

"It's ok, Seamus. It was a damned ugly thing. If our situations had been reversed, it would probably take me a little while to get over the shock of it too."

Seamus started to object, but I couldn't bear to hear him contradict me, because I didn't want to know what I already suspected: that if he had been holding the gun, he never would have pulled the trigger, or only would have pulled it too late. So I kissed him, partially to stop him from saying anything, and partially to prove to us both that we were still human. That we were still capable of something as normal and life-affirming as a kiss. I probably should have asked first, but with the way he leaned into it and pulled me closer, I figured my lapse was forgivable.

Of course, it was in that moment that Sol burst through the door to the cupboard that we'd been searching through.

"Oh! Sorry to interrupt. I figured you'd want your sandwiches."

Seamus and I both laughed as we pulled apart.

"Sandwiches sound like a great idea," I said, while Seamus simply replied by taking a giant bite out of the slab of bread and meat offered to him.

I had just taken a bite of mine, and was opening my mouth to exclaim that Sol was officially the one and only sandwich-maker-in-chief as far as I was concerned, when Gwen popped into existence right behind Sol's back and shouted, "They're coming! Hurry up! Get Seamus out of here!"

"Gwen, what!? Who's coming? What the hell is—"

But she was already gone, as were Sol and Trev, as Seamus and I realized as soon as we stepped out of the cupboard and into the kitchen.

Seamus ran to the door to check the lock and look out the window.

"What the fuck?" he asked, taking the words right out of my mouth.

"Did Gwen just nab Sol and Trev?" I asked.

He nodded, crossing towards the living room window, probably to see if MOME was within sight.

I started to follow, in case we needed to make a quick exit.

"I guess we'd better get out of he—"

Then the door exploded in a rain of fire and wood, and I was leaping behind the kitchen island, screaming Seamus' name. I could hear boots hitting the floor and shouts filling the air, so I shifted to where I'd last seen Seamus before the door exploded, hoping that I could shift us out, but Seamus wasn't near the window, he was on the floor next to the couch (which was only reasonable as the air was filled with ricocheting spells of every variety). I reached down to grab him so we could get the fuck out of Dodge, but then something hot hit my back and I was screaming in pain, and Seamus was screaming something, and then the world went black.

“**O**W. FUCK.”

“Thank gods, you’re awake.”

“Seamus?”

I had to ask, because it was pitch black in… wherever the hell we were. I could feel a hard surface underneath my shoulder and leg, and I seemed to be lying on my left side. Other than that, I had no clue what was going on, except that I could hear Seamus’ voice, and half my body felt like it was on fire and/or had been hit by a truck— mostly and.

“Are you ok?” Seamus' voice asked.

“I don’t know. I’m afraid to try to move, because just lying here hurts enough as it is. What the fuck happened?”

“MOME got us.”

"Yeah, I guessed that much. But what *happened?* How did they find us? Why aren't we dead? And where the seven fucks are we?"

"Do you mean before or after you killed a MOME agent?"

"After. I remember that part. And we aren't sure that I killed him. He could have lived if they got him help soon enough."

I wasn't happy about the reminder of how I had shot a man in the chest at point-blank range, but I was in too much pain to notice the nausea that rose when I thought about it, so that was something… I guess.

"I don't know how they found us, except that we were at your house, so I suppose they must have known where to look. Do you remember Gwen coming and grabbing Sol and Trev?"

"Yeah, it's the stuff after that part that's… fuzzy."

"Well, after that you jumped behind the kitchen island and I dove to the floor, then you shifted to me, I assume to take us somewhere else, but they were waiting for that, or else they had just decided to start firing everywhere at once, and you got hit, and… I don't know why they didn't kill us, but they threw us in the back of a truck and… then they dropped us here. They put bags on both our heads.

Not sure why they bothered with yours, since you've been out cold from the moment they hit you with that spell, but all I saw was when they put the hood on your scorched, unconscious form, and since then I have literally been in the dark."

"How long have I been out?" I asked, trying to think past the pain all down the right side of my body, as well as the headache that was quickly taking up residence inside my skull.

"I'm not sure. It's not like they've been coming in to tell me the time and date, but… a few days, at any rate."

"Days?! Was I in a coma?"

"Kinda. I think. I don't know. Honestly, Vic, I seriously thought I was never going to talk to you again."

Seamus sounded like he was about to cry, or maybe like he had been crying for a while already. It was hard to tell. His voice was rough, at any rate, and I couldn't say I blamed him. I wasn't exactly feeling like this situation was made of win as it was, and if he had thought me as good as dead for a few days…

"Any idea what kind of spell they hit me with?" I asked, mainly to get us both thinking about something other than how screwed we probably were.

"No idea. I don't have much experience with mages at all…. Now, if a giant were had mauled you, I could probably be of more help."

I tried to laugh, but it hurt too much.

"Ow."

"Sorry."

"No, it's good. If we don't keep up a sense of humor, then we're fucked."

Seamus chuckled.

"Oh, good to know there's still hope, then."

"There's always hope, Seamus."

"Yeah. If you say so, Vic. Any chance you'll be able to walk soon?"

I took a moment to assess. My right side was still alight with pain. It was an awful combination of the hot pain of a bad burn and the dull ache of a strong impact. I tried to move my right arm, but the immediate response from my nervous system was to abandon ship. I took multiple deep breaths to keep from passing out, then decided that I would wait a bit before I tried my right leg. I needed to rest up first.

"Not likely," I replied, after conducting my little mobility test. "But I don't really need to be able to walk, do I?"

Seamus didn't say anything for a moment.

"Wherever we are, I can't pull on my wolf form."

"Well shit. I suppose there's a null somewhere nearby, then."

"Maybe."

"How long did it take them to bring us here?"

"I dunno. Long enough that they stopped to let me pee once along the way."

"So they brought us by car?"

"Yeah."

"Weird. What did they do about me?"

"Can't you smell yourself?"

Ugh... I couldn't. Either because my nose was just used to it, after however long we'd been like this, or maybe because I'd been damaged somehow. Fuck. I hope I hadn't lost my sense of smell, that would suck.

"I'm just kidding. You're either super dehydrated, or they have a spell for that, or something."

"You ass."

"You said we needed to keep our senses of humor."

"I hate you."

"That's fair."

And then I tried to laugh again, and wound up almost crying, because it hurt so damned much.

"Owwww... ok. No more sense of humor, it's going to kill me."

"Vic, how do we get out of this?"

"I don't know." I thought about that for a long time. I wasn't touching Seamus right now, so I couldn't shift us both, but to be honest, I wouldn't have tried anyway. Beyond the fact that there was a null somewhere nearby, which likely made it impossible anyway, I felt so wrecked by whatever had happened to me that, judging by how much energy shifting had taken from me in the past, I didn't think I would be able to move the two of us for quite some time.

"This must be episode two," I muttered.

"What?" Seamus asked.

"Episode two. You know, in episode one the plucky, brave underdog is pulled into a world he or she doesn't understand, but manages to gain the upper hand somehow. In episode two, everything falls apart, and it looks like our hero is lost."

"And then in episode three the plucky underdog takes it all back and wins the day?"

"Yep. Everyone's favorite fiction trope."

"Right… so, how do we get to episode three?"

"Close our eyes and wait for rescue?" I suggested, half-heartedly.

And with that, I did close my eyes, since having them open didn't seem to make any difference anyway. Seamus remained silent too, and, eventually, sleep took me.

Vic's adventures continue in *Victoria Marmot and the Shadow of Death* (out now)!
Victoria Marmot Books 4 is coming soon!

The Chronicles of Gensokai Series:
Blade's Edge
Traitor's Hope

Short stories:
Rain on a Summer's Afternoon

Follow Virginia on social media:
www.virginiamcclain.com
twitter.com/gwendamned
facebook.com/virginiamcclainauthor

ACKNOWLEDGEMENTS

These books wouldn't have been possible without a fair bit of help from a number of people. My deepest gratitude goes out to the following people:

My editor, Aurora Wilson-McClain, for not only working with my sometimes ridiculous deadlines, but also for helping me sort out the best use of obscure spell references, the number of "s"s a certain dragon uses in her speech patterns, and where, exactly, everyone has left their clothes.

My husband, for putting up with me disappearing every evening for months on end in order to get these books written, for being my best cheerleader and for not giving me too much grief when I failed to get my half of the housework done.

Cedar, for letting me ignore her often enough to get formatting done, as well as promotion and marketing stuff, and for being so willing to hang out with her wonderful caregivers.

Anne, Lee, Jim, and Gabi, for keeping Cedar entertained, fed, and happy so that I could write.

To my Patreon supporters: Paul, Corey, Mishy, and Jessica.

And finally, the folks at Stella's au CCFM for always putting up with me occupying a table for hours on end while only ordering a cup of tea.

Virginia McClain is an author who masqueraded as a language teacher for a decade or so. When she's not reading or writing she can generally be found playing outside with her four legged adventure buddy and the tiny human she helped to build from scratch. She enjoys climbing to the tops of tall rocks, running through deserts, mountains, and woodlands, and carrying a foldable home on her back whenever she gets a chance. She's also fond of word games, and writing descriptions of herself that are needlessly vague.

For more information check out

www.virginiamcclain.com

facebook.com/virginiamcclainauthor

twitter.com/gwendamned

bookbub.com/author/virginia-mcclain